JO SEAGAR'S
Easy Peasy
SUMMER ENTERTAINING

PHOTOGRAPHY BY JOHN DALEY

cumulus

Acknowledgements

My sincere appreciation and thanks to my dear friend John Daley, who is such a wonderful photographer and all-round good guy.

To Helen Jackson, my assistant extraordinaire — she cooks, she types, she tests recipes, and her food styling abilities are exceptional.

To Jamie Wright for all his wonderful computer work and general assistance, and, yes, help with tasting the recipes too!

To Maree O'Neill, make-up artist and stylist, for all the help with the cover shot and for being such a good friend.

To my husband Ross (or 'Denis' as he calls himself now). Thank you for your wonderful help and support.

To Katie and Guy, for being so good and not playing on the computer while the 'work in progress' sign was up.

And a special thank you to my dear mother Fay, for always being there when I need her — which is often!

Published 1998 by Cumulus for
Whitcoulls Ltd
210 Queen St
Auckland

© 1998 Jo Seagar (text), John Daley (photographs)

ISBN 1 86954 506 0

Design by Christine Cathie
Printed in New Zealand

Contents

Introduction

Maximum effect with minimal effort has always been, and will always remain, my cooking philosophy. And to survive the summer holidays I have worked out a strategy, using recipes and cunning entertaining tips, that takes this philosophy to its most advanced state. Life is busy and full, and I for one am just not prepared to put all my time and effort into entertaining when there are so many other fun things I want to do.

Don't get me wrong — I adore having friends over, and I love to feed and water them with style and panache — but like most people I don't count sous-chefs and kitchenhands among my household, so I leave most of the tiddly fiddly culinary manoeuvres to restaurants and catering companies, with their back-up casts of thousands.

But — that doesn't mean the results are anything less than 'knock em for six' impressive. I want to give really memorable dinner parties that will have my friends and family talking about the 'great party, wonderful food' for months — hopefully (12 months) until we do it all again. But I don't want to become a victim of my own hospitality — where perhaps my guests had a great time but how would I know — I didn't get a chance to chat to them (or catch up on all the goss) because I was stuck over the proverbial hot stove in the kitchen while everyone else was having fun and games in the sunshine.

There has to be a better way. I think the answer to surviving the holiday season is to prepare ahead and to stagger preparations. What with card writing and Christmas shopping, filling the tins and making presents, school break-ups and tree trimming, it's busy enough as it is, while fixing a date that fits into everyone's diary is a small triumph in itself. You've got to be a list-keeper and a 'ticker offer' of these lists, otherwise the only staggering you'll be doing is through your own party. (Oh, how I've always wanted to be one of those organised people — buy it in August, wrap it in September kind of gal — but I've never got quite that efficient.)

However, if you have heaps of taste and style (which I know you have because you're reading this book) and you enjoy entertaining but only have limited time (surely that covers everyone), well this is the book for you.

'Easy Peasy' recipes that work, recipes you can fling together without complicated instructions or equipment. I've used mainly cups and spoons for measurements, and I think that in only one recipe do you have to sift the flour and that can be through an old kitchen strainer. I've made maximum use of my own little team of helpers, and I'm talking the microwave, blender and food processor here — not 'the staff'.

While I'm emphasising that these recipes are for holiday entertaining there are plenty of everyday dishes in here too, but really we're talking party time — Christmas, New Year's Day and all the special occasions when you really want to show off.

We're pushing the extremes of moderation here. There's so much more to food than just fuel, and I think of these special-occasion recipes as soul food. Maybe the love content is matched by the fat content but, hey, it's party time, and who's counting?

There are heaps of helpful tips and easy recipes here, so there's no need to panic at the prospect of entertaining. And after all, it's only dinner. Nothing dreadful is going to happen because you've bought the dessert and haven't been slaving over pots and pans for weeks. Just because a recipe is full of French terminology, written in complicated jargon, used every piece of cooking paraphernalia you own and taken hours to execute doesn't automatically mean a fabulously successful dinner party. And, most importantly, I don't care what you're wearing, dark circles under the eyes and yawning is not a good look with any outfit.

So read on for my clever (some would say cheating) ideas and survival recipes, all written for busy and harassed cooks who want to serve impressive dishes to their friends and guests but, like me, are not prepared to lay their lives down for the cause.

One last thing — guard against that ole demon modesty — it's very unbecoming in the cook. When your guests shower you with extravagant praise about the delicious food and how clever you are, don't go straight onto autopilot and say, 'Oh, it was nothing' or 'It was so easy, I just added a tub of sour cream and a jar of store-bought pickle.' STOP! Practise saying just 'Thank you.' You *are* the clever one, for knowing all the tricks and how to take the shortcuts — happily accept that praise as your due.

Cooking and entertaining can be marvellous fun. In fact I think it is one of life's greatest pleasures, feeding and nurturing the people you love and enjoy being with. So my wish to you is, may *every* holiday season be stuffed full with tidings of comfort and joy!

Nibbles and Food for Drinks Parties

Crostini

Makes 30 from one loaf of French bread

day-old French bread stick
olive oil spray or olive oil to brush
garlic salt

Slice the French stick into 5 mm thick slices. Spray a baking tray liberally with olive oil, and on it place a single layer of bread slices. Liberally spray or brush the slices of bread with olive oil and sprinkle with garlic salt.

Bake at 180°C for 10–15 minutes, until crisp and golden; watch carefully as they tend to burn quickly. Cool on a wire rack and store in an airtight container.

Topping Ideas

I like to spread crostini with cream cheese before adding other toppings. This moistens them and provides a good base for the toppings. Be quite generous with the cream cheese — don't scrape it on meanly like Marmite.

Top with:
- Char-grilled peppers and olive tapenade with parsley sprigs.
- Smoked salmon and caviar.
- Prawns and lemon pepper seasoning.
- Avocado and pastrami.
- Smoked chicken and mango chutney.
- Smoked zucchini and fresh basil.

Crostini with char-grilled pepper and tapenade

Seasoned Potato Wedges

Serves 4

A great drinks-party food for dips, best served piping hot.

4 medium potatoes
¼ cup olive oil
garlic salt and freshly ground black pepper
½ teaspoon paprika or cajun spice mix
spray oil, or additional oil to drizzle

Cut each potato into 8 wedges. Place in a large bowl and soak in cold water for 15 minutes. Drain the potatoes and dry them off with a paper towel, then return them to the bowl. Add the olive oil, garlic salt, freshly ground black pepper and paprika or cajun spice, and mix (I find it best to get dirty and mix by hand).

Spray an oven tray with oil, or drizzle over a little olive oil, place the wedges on the tray and bake for 40–45 minutes at 180°C. Spray or drizzle the wedges with oil and turn them occasionally so that they cook on both sides. The wedges should be crisp on the outside and light and fluffy on the inside.

Left to right; hummus, sour cream and green gherkin, beetroot and horseradish, tarragon aoli, piccalli dip

Thai Dip

Makes 2 cups

150 g sour cream
½ cup coconut milk
1 teaspoon crushed garlic
1 tablespoon sweet chilli sauce
2 tablespoons each of coriander, parsley and mint, chopped
a squeeze of lemon or lime

Mix all the ingredients together and season with salt and freshly ground black pepper. Chill and serve with crackers, raw vegetables, crostini, etc.

Tarragon Aioli

Makes 1½ cups

2 egg yolks
1 teaspoon hot smooth English mustard
1–2 cloves garlic, crushed (1 teaspoon)
juice and grated rind of 1 lemon
300 ml olive oil
2 tablespoons chopped fresh tarragon
salt and freshly ground black pepper

Place the yolks, mustard, garlic and lemon juice in a blender or food processor. Run the machine for 30 seconds until well combined, scraping down the sides of the bowl as required. Gradually pour in a thin stream of olive oil (almost a teaspoon at a time); the mixture will thicken. Add the tarragon and season to taste, cover and chill until required.

Serve with a platter of fresh baby vegetables. The firmer ones like carrots and cauliflower should be blanched in boiling water for a minute or two then refreshed in cold water to keep them crisp and colourful.

Beetroot and Horseradish Salsa

Makes 2 cups

Simple Dips

These dips are speedy to prepare but your guests will think you've been in the kitchen for hours chopping, shredding and blending ingredients. A total cheat, but worth heaps of 'Brownie points'.

250 g sour cream or thick creamy yoghurt
½ cup green gherkin relish or piccalilli pickle or chutney
2 tablespoons chopped parsley or any fresh herb — coriander, chives etc.

Mix together and keep in the fridge, covered, until required. (Makes 2 cups.)

1 × 400 g can baby beetroot, drained
3 large pickled gherkins
2 tablespoons olive oil
2 tablespoons horseradish sauce
salt and freshly ground black pepper

Finely chop the beetroot and gherkins. Mix with the olive oil and horseradish sauce, season with salt and freshly ground black pepper, and chill. Store covered in the fridge for a day or two.

Hummus

Makes 1½ cups

1 × 425 g can chickpeas, drained (reserve liquid)
2 cloves garlic, crushed (1 teaspoon)
juice and grated rind of 2 lemons
5 tablespoons tahini (sesame paste)
½ teaspoon ground cumin
2 tablespoons olive oil

Process the chickpeas, garlic, lemon juice, grated rind, tahini and cumin until smooth, then add the chickpea liquid or water to make a thick mayonnaise consistency. Drizzle in the olive oil and season to taste. Serve on crostini, garnished with olives, chopped parsley or sliced red pepper.

Tarragon aioli

9

Christmas Tree-shaped Cheese Biscuits

Makes about 36

150 g butter
250 g grated tasty cheese
1½ cups flour
salt and freshly ground black pepper

Optional Extras

- crushed corn chips or potato chips
- sesame or poppy seeds
- crushed cardamom
- lemon pepper seasoning
- cajun spice
- sea-salt flakes or coarsely ground rock salt
- celery seeds

Mix all the ingredients in a food processor, adding any of the optional extra flavourings. With floured hands roll into a ball. Then roll out flat, and with a Christmas tree cookie cutter (or other fancy shape) press out little tree shapes. Place on a sheet of baking paper on an oven tray and chill in the fridge for 30 minutes. Sesame seeds, poppy seeds, rock salt, etc. can be pressed into the surface of each biscuit.

Bake for 15 minutes at (180°C) until golden brown. Cool for 2–3 minutes on the tray then slide onto a wire rack to cool completely. Store in airtight containers.

Shrimp 'Soldiers'

Serves 4–6

6–8 slices thick white toast sliced bread, preferably a few days old
6–10 medium prawns, peeled and uncooked
2 spring onions, finely chopped
2 tablespoons sesame oil
1 teaspoon grated fresh ginger
salt and freshly ground black pepper
1 egg white
2 teaspoons cornflour
3 tablespoons sesame seeds
oil for deep-frying
sweet chilli sauce, to serve

Remove the crusts from the toasting bread and cut into finger-like 'soldiers'. Roughly chop the prawns and place them in a food processor with the spring onions, sesame oil, ginger, salt, freshly ground black pepper, egg white and cornflour. Process until the mixture forms a smooth paste, then spread the mixture thickly over each piece of bread, smoothing the edges. Sprinkle with sesame seeds. Fry in hot oil, filling-side down, until golden brown. Remove and drain on paper towels. Serve immediately accompanied by sweet chilli sauce.

Gruyère, Walnut and Rosemary Wafers

Makes about 14

1 cup grated gruyère cheese
½ cup chopped walnuts
1 tablespoon fresh rosemary leaves, chopped

Line a baking sheet with baking paper or a teflon sheet. Divide the grated cheese into 12–14 small rounds, each about 5 cm in diameter, and sprinkle with the walnuts and rosemary. Bake at 180°C for 4–5 minutes, until golden and melted. Cool on a wire rack.

Old-fashioned Mousetraps

Makes 30

10 slices sandwich bread
1½ cups grated cheese
2 eggs, beaten
1 teaspoon (or good slosh) Worcester sauce
1 teaspoon grainy mustard
salt and freshly ground black pepper to taste
6–8 rashers rindless streaky bacon, chopped or snipped into little
  pieces

Trim the crusts off the bread slices (if you want to). Mix all the other ingredients together and spread over the bread. Cut each slice into 3 'soldiers' and bake at 200°C for 10–15 minutes, until the topping is golden and puffed and the toast crisp and dry.

Tiny Bread Cases

1 loaf thinly sliced sandwich bread, brown or white or a mixture
oil spray

Using a round cookie cutter approximately 3–4 cm in diameter, cut out two rounds from each slice of bread. Carefully press the bread rounds into deep mini-muffin trays and spray with oil. Place a second tray on top (to keep the bread-case shape) and bake at 180°C for 10–15 minutes, until crisp and golden. Cool on a wire rack and store in an airtight container until required.

Suggested Fillings
- Pan-fried button mushrooms with crème fraîche and fresh sage.
- Cream cheese with smoked oysters, garnished with a sprig of dill.
- Pesto topped with cherry tomatoes.
- Prawns and tomato with mayonnaise.
- Baby scallops marinated in lime juice with coconut cream.
- Smoked salmon and cream cheese topped with caviar.

Cream cheese with smoked oyster

Black caviar and wasabi caviar

Spicy Popcorn Noodle Mix

Makes 8 cups

1 kg raw nuts — a mixture of peanuts, hazelnuts, almonds,
*   cashews, macadamias, pecans, walnuts, etc.*
2 tablespoons oil
3 tablespoons mild curry powder or prepared curry paste
approx. 4 cups ready-to-eat caramel-flavoured popcorn (3 × 50 g
*   packets)*
approx. 4 cups ready-to-eat crispy noodles (2 × 140 g packets
*   High Mark noodles)*

Toss the nuts in the oil and curry powder and roast for 35–40 minutes at 180°C, stirring often. Cool and mix in the caramel popcorn and crispy noodles. Season with salt to taste. Store in an airtight container and serve within 2–3 days.

Mini 'Toad in the Hole'

Makes 60

Great finger food for a drinks party.

8–10 thin pre-cooked sausages (sizzlers, chipolatas, etc.)
1 cup flour
450 ml milk
4 tablespoons grainy mustard
2 eggs
salt and freshly ground black pepper
non-stick oil cooking spray

Cut the sausages into little pieces small enough to fit into mini muffin tins. In a blender or food processor mix the flour, milk, mustard and eggs with salt and freshly ground black pepper to taste. Spray deep non-stick mini-muffin tins with oil spray. Place a piece of sausage in each cup and bake at 200°C for 10 minutes, until they are starting to turn golden brown.

Pour approximately 1 tablespoon of batter over each piece of sausage and return to the oven to cook for a further 15–20 minutes, until puffed and golden. Serve immediately, with a chutney or finely chopped salsa as a dipping sauce.

Sushi Rice Balls

Makes 30–35

¾ cups sushi-zu (special sushi rice vinegar — see note)
3 cups cooked sushi-style rice (see note)
2 tablespoons black sesame seeds
2 tablespoons toasted sesame seeds

Note: To prepare sushi-style rice cook shortgrain Japanese rice by the sticky method, either in a rice cooker or boiled in 3 cups of salted water until all the water is absorbed.

If you have trouble finding prepared sushi-zu vinegar, it can be made by mixing together 1 tablespoon sugar, 1 teaspoon salt, ¼ cup sherry or rice wine and ¼ cup rice vinegar.

Mix the sushi-zu vinegar through the warm sushi rice, toss well and cool. Roll into small balls. Mix the black and toasted sesame seeds on a tray and roll the sticky rice balls in the sesame seeds. Cover with plastic wrap and chill until required.

Serve with soy sauce mixed, if desired, with a little wasabi (green Japanese horseradish paste).

Little Frypan Sandwiches

Make sandwiches as normal using thick white toast-sliced bread, or 5 mm thick slices of French bread. Spread with grainy mustard, shaved or thinly sliced ham and slices of tasty cheese, thin tomato slices and large basil leaves.

Butter the outsides of the bread as well, and cook in a large frypan until golden brown, about 4 minutes each side. This allows the cheese to melt deliciously inside.

Cut into small bite-size pieces and serve warm.

Bacon, Tomato and Avocado-filled Croissants

Small croissants, split and heated briefly in the oven, make a great easy-to-eat brunch. Fill with crisp bacon (cooked in the oven), sliced tomato and ripe avocado. Sprinkle with salt and freshly ground black pepper and pass around wrapped in napkins.

Little frypan sandwiches

Small Courses

Roast Pepper and Ricotta Loaf

Makes 1 large loaf, 10–12 slices

1 kg ricotta cheese
200 g grated parmesan cheese
6 eggs
1½ teaspoons salt
freshly ground white pepper
½ cup finely chopped Italian parsley
2 tablespoons finely chopped oregano
4–5 char-grilled or roasted pepper halves (Kato brand are
available in vacuum packs or jars)
1 teaspoon extra virgin olive oil
paprika

Mix the ricotta, parmesan, eggs, salt and pepper together in a food processor, then pour half the mixture into an oiled loaf tin (30 × 12 × 7 cm). Sprinkle over the chopped herbs, then add a layer of char-grilled pepper. Pour over the remaining mixture. Drizzle the surface with oil and dust with paprika.

Bake at 160°C for an hour; the loaf will puff up then settle down again. Cool in the fridge.

Serve with roasted tomato, pickles, bread, salad leaves, etc. This loaf is great for serving a large number of guests as a first course.

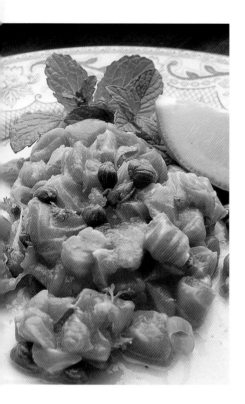

Lemon- and Vodka-marinated Salmon with Capers

Serves 4–6

1 medium-size fresh salmon (approx. 750 g)
5 spring onions, finely chopped
3 tablespoons drained capers
½ cup chopped mint
3 tablespoons vodka
3 tablespoons extra virgin olive oil
grated rind and juice of 1 large lemon
salt and freshly ground black pepper

Fillet, skin and bone the salmon; cut it into small pieces. Combine all the ingredients and refrigerate overnight. Serve with triangles of wholemeal toast or crostini with cream cheese, or on its own as a delicious little salmon salad.

Hot Pasta — Cold Tomato

Such a simple dish, this is an absolute winner and a big favourite of mine — it's my standard speedy summertime meal.

tomatoes, sliced (preferably big beefy or Roma)
drizzle olive oil
splash white-wine vinegar
lots of salt and freshly ground black pepper
chopped basil or parsley
pasta
parmesan cheese

Make a bowl of fresh tomato salad (preferably sun-ripened, just picked, etc.); i.e. sliced tomatoes with olive oil, white-wine vinegar and salt and freshly ground black pepper, plus some chopped basil or parsley.

Boil pasta, any sort — I particularly like a penne type because it's easy to eat, but fettuccine or spaghetti are just fine. As soon as the pasta is tender, drain and toss it with the tomato salad, then pick up your fork and go!

A little shaved parmesan is a nice touch, and a piece of crusty bread on the side is perfect to mop up the juices.

Pasta with Grilled Asparagus, Broad Beans and Lemon

Serves 4

500 g asparagus
2 cups shelled broad beans (frozen are fine)
350 g dried penne pasta or other
100 ml extra virgin olive oil
2 cloves garlic, crushed (1 teaspoon)
grated rind and juice of 1 lemon
3 teaspoons chopped fresh mint
100 ml cream
½ cup freshly grated parmesan cheese
salt and freshly ground black pepper

Trim the asparagus and slice in half lengthways. Place the asparagus in a grill pan (or on the barbecue), brush with a little oil and grill for 3–4 minutes on each side, until charred and tender.

Blanch the beans in lightly salted water for 2 minutes, then remove with a sieve. Refresh the beans in cold water and remove the hard outer skin. Return the bean water to a rolling boil, add the pasta and cook for about 10 minutes, until just tender.

Meanwhile, heat the oil, add the crushed garlic and lemon rind, and fry gently for 3 minutes. Add the beans, mint and cream, and heat gently.

Drain the pasta and toss with the asparagus and the bean sauce. Stir in the cheese and lemon juice to taste. Season and serve in a warm bowl.

Parmesan Baskets of Roast Pear, Blue Cheese and Toasted-walnut Salad

fresh parmesan, shaved or grated (not the processed powdery variety); allow ½ a cup per basket
firm green pears; allow ½ a pear per serving
lettuce and a selection of salad leaves
soft blue cheese, e.g. Blue Castello or blue brie
3–4 toasted walnuts per serving; about 50 g for 4 servings
croûtons and crisp bacon (optional)
1 tablespoon vinaigrette dressing per serving (with perhaps a dash of Cointreau or Grand Marnier in the dressing)

The baskets will keep for 2–3 days in an airtight container. If they go soft give them a few minutes (placed over the original mould to keep their shape) in a medium oven (180°C) to crisp up.

To make the parmesan baskets, line an oven tray with baking paper or a teflon sheet. Sprinkle the parmesan in rounds about the size of a bread and butter plate. Bake at 160°C for around 10 minutes. Remove from the oven and mould into shape over an upturned bowl, or a cup without a handle, leave until cool.

Peel and core the pears, drizzle with olive oil and roast in a hot oven (200°C) for 20–25 minutes until golden and soft.

Place the parmesan baskets on serving plates and fill with a selection of lettuce and salad leaves. Slice the pears and the blue cheese and divide among the baskets. Add the walnuts, croûtons and bacon if desired, and sprinkle with dressing. Serve immediately.

Avocado with Smoked Salmon and Caviar

Serves 4

An impressive first course that is easy to prepare and a good way to serve just a tiny bit of seafood to a number of guests (for example 1 small crayfish for 6 people).

Variations

All sorts of variations are possible using different salad leaves or sprouts as the base. Different seafoods, such as shrimps, crayfish meat or smoked fish, can also be used for the filling, and different herbs and garnishes.

2 perfect avocados, firm but ripe

alfalfa sprouts, chopped cucumber or salad leaves

150 g sour cream or flavoured dip (the green gherkin relish and sour cream dip is extra good)

50–100 g smoked salmon slices (or substitute crayfish, prawns, etc.)

3 teaspoons caviar or smoked salmon roe

herb sprigs

vinaigrette

Slice the avocados in half lengthways; remove and discard the stones. Sit each avocado half on a bed of alfalfa sprouts, chopped cucumber or salad greens. Spoon a little sour cream into the stone cavity then garnish with a swirl of smoked salmon and a dollop of caviar — remember, only use a little bit of caviar, and they'll think it's real (Jo's food psychology). Add herb sprigs of your choice and serve with a little classic vinaigrette to the side.

Aubergine Rolls with Tomato Jam

Serves 4

Tomato Jam

1 × 400 g can peeled tomatoes in juice
2 tablespoons balsamic or red wine vinegar
salt and freshly ground black pepper

To make the tomato jam, chop the tomatoes and simmer them (and their juice) and the balsamic vinegar for 30 minutes, uncovered, stirring often. Pass the mixture through a sieve, season with salt and freshly ground black pepper, and reduce by further simmering until it is the consistency of a sauce.

2–3 large aubergines (eggplants), sliced lengthways into 5 mm strips
approx. ¼ cup olive oil
150 g spreadable cream cheese
approx. 70 g feta cheese, crumbled
3 tablespoons chopped flat-leaved parsley

Heat oil in a large pan and fry the aubergine slices until they are softened and golden coloured on both sides. Cool on a wire rack. Mix the softened cream cheese and the feta until smooth (this can be done in a food processor), then spread the mixture over the aubergine slices (like buttering toast). Add a layer of tomato jam, sprinkle with chopped parsley, roll up and chill.

To serve, slice the rolls (like sushi), spoon over a little tomato jam, and garnish with fresh salad leaves and herbs. Smaller pieces can be served as nibbles.

Glorified Bacon and Egg Pie

Serves 10–12

4 sheets flaky puff pastry
4 cups grated cheese
10–12 rashers lean bacon, chopped, 6–8 cold barbecue sausages
  or 2 cups chopped ham pieces
5 spring onions, sliced
2 cups sliced mushrooms (approx. 250 g)
2 cups sliced zucchini or peas, beans, corn, etc. (frozen are fine)
½ cup chopped parsley or fresh herbs of your choice
1 cup chutney, relish or pickle
salt and freshly ground black pepper to taste
12 eggs

Join the sheets of pastry together in a big square — I wet each edge with water then crimp it with a fork to really seal the join. Lay the pastry in a large, non-stick pie plate or frypan, etc; the pastry hanging over the sides will be folded back to enclose the filling. I use a large non-stick pan which has a handle that can safely go in the oven. Sprinkle the pastry in the pan with cheese to waterproof it.

Layer up the cheese, bacon (or sausages or ham pieces), vegetables, herbs, chutney or relish, seasoning as you go. Break the eggs over the filling, piercing the yolks (reserving half a yolk to glaze).

Fold the edges of the pastry over, enclosing the filling completely. Wet the joins and seal them, using a patchwork technique with the pastry if necessary. Whisk the reserved egg yolk with 1 tablespoon of cold water and brush the pastry generously with this mixture.

Bake at 200°C for 35 minutes, until golden and puffed, then turn the oven temperature down to 180°C and bake for a further 45–50 minutes. Cool for about an hour in the pan then ease out onto a board. Serve warm or at room temperature, or it can be reheated later. Pies like this freeze well.

Barbecue Scallops in the Shell with White Wine and Garlic Butter

First catch your scallops. Ideally this recipe should use shellfish no older than 10 minutes from the sea.

scallops
garlic
butter
white wine
black pepper

Mix up a little bowl of garlic butter — no accurate measurements here, just add as much garlic as you like, approximately 1 teaspoon of garlic to 200 g butter.

Clean the scallops of the yucky black and brown bits, so only the orange and white parts remain. Give the scallop shells a good scrub in seawater and put two or three scallops in each. Place a small knob of garlic butter on top of the scallops (about a teaspoonful), add a couple of tablespoons of white wine and a good grind of black pepper.

Carefully place the shells on the barbecue grill and cook for a few minutes only. The scallop meat should just turn white and the butter melt into the wine — any longer and the scallops can turn quite rubbery and shrink. Even when they are removed from the grill the liquid poaches them for a moment or so longer. Now you're in for a taste sensation. Eat, enjoy, and don't forget to drink the divine juices, or mop them up with crusty bread.

Oysters

Oysters should smell fresh and of the sea. They shouldn't be slimy, but glossy, plump and clear. Oysters on the half shell freeze really well with little loss of texture, plumpness or flavour. Quickly thaw the oysters by placing them in salted fresh water, then serve them either 'au naturel' with a squeeze of lemon and freshly ground black pepper or in one of these ways.

Oriental Dressing for Oysters

¼ cup rice wine vinegar

2 teaspoons soy sauce

1 teaspoon sweet chilli sauce

juice and grated rind of a lemon

1 teaspoon minced ginger

1 spring onion, green part only, finely sliced

Mix all the ingredients together in a bowl and serve as a dipping sauce, or drizzle over the oysters.

Oysters with Lemon Pepper Crumbs

4 slices toast bread

1 teaspoon lemon pepper

½ teaspoon paprika

50 g melted butter

lemon or lime juice

parsley, to garnish

Process the bread to crumbs in a food processor and add the lemon pepper, paprika and butter. Squeeze a little lemon or lime juice over each oyster on the half shell, and top with the crumb mixture. Place under a hot grill for 3–4 minutes and garnish with parsley.

Mustard Dill Cream

1 tablespoon smooth Dijon-style mustard

150 g sour cream (approx. 1 small cup)

1 tablespoon chopped fresh dill and dill sprigs, to garnish

Mix together and place a teaspoonful on each oyster on the half shell; garnish with a sprig of dill.

Sweetcorn and Zucchini Fritters

Serves 4

1 × 310 g can cream-style sweetcorn
2–3 zucchini, grated (approx. 1 cup)
¾ cup self-raising flour
¼ cup milk
2 eggs, separated
salt and freshly ground black pepper
1 teaspoon sweet chilli sauce
50 g butter and 3 tablespoons oil, to cook

Serve with crisp bacon or sausages and a green salad, or simply with a dollop of sour cream and sweet chilli sauce.

In a bowl mix together the cream-style corn, grated zucchini, self-raising flour, milk, egg yolks, salt, freshly ground black pepper and sweet chilli sauce. In a separate small bowl beat the egg whites until stiff. Fold the egg whites into the mixture.

Melt the butter and oil in a non-stick pan and cook spoonfuls of the mixture over a medium heat for about 3 minutes. Drain on paper towels.

Gazpacho — Summer Chilled Tomato Soup

Serves 4–6

2 large tomatoes, chopped finely
1 large cucumber, peeled, halved lengthways and seeds removed
1 large onion, finely chopped
1 large roasted, peeled red pepper (Kato brand are available in
*   vacuum packs or jars)*
3 cups tomato juice
2 stalks celery, finely sliced
½ cup chopped fresh coriander
¼ cup red wine vinegar
¼ cup olive oil
a few drops of hot pepper sauce (Kaitaia Fire or tabasco)
1 teaspoon Worcester sauce
salt and freshly ground black pepper
parsley, to garnish

Place 1 tomato, half the cucumber, half the onion, the red pepper and the tomato juice in a blender and purée. Transfer to a bowl and add all the remaining ingredients. Check the seasoning and add salt and freshly ground black pepper accordingly. Refrigerate and serve chilled; garnish with fresh parsley. Gazpacho can be prepared 2–3 days ahead.

Blue Cheese Pasta

Serves 4

*400 g (approx. 3 cups) dried penne pasta, or 500 g fresh tortellini
    or ravioli*
50 g butter
5 spring onions, finely sliced
1 cup cream or milk (low-fat milk works fine)
250 g blue cheese
* salt and freshly ground black pepper*
½ cup coarsely chopped parsley
1 cup chopped nuts if desired; walnuts, toasted hazelnuts, etc.

Cook the pasta in a large saucepan of boiling salted water; the time will vary according to the type of pasta — follow the directions on the packet. Drain, melt the butter in the hot saucepan, add the spring onions and cook for 30–40 seconds. Add the cream or milk and crumble in the blue cheese — I love a soft blue Castello cheese but use any blue cheese you like. Stir until mostly melted. Season with salt and freshly ground black pepper (lots of pepper, but watch the salt as the cheese can be quite salty). Add the parsley and nuts and return the pasta to the saucepan; toss gently and serve immediately with lots of crusty bread to mop up the gorgeous juices.

Main Courses

Lasagne Pasta Rolls with Shaved Ham and Parmesan

Serves 6–8

1 packet fresh lasagne sheets
2 cups shaved parmesan
250 g shredded ham (a couple of big handfuls)
3 cloves garlic, crushed (1 teaspoon)
300 ml cream
2 × 400 g cans tomatoes in juice (or crushed tomatoes and onion)
½ cup white wine
2 cups sliced button mushrooms
approx. ½ cup black olives, pitted
1 cup mozzarella cheese
tomato, flat-leaf parsley, basil, to garnish

Cut the lasagne sheets in half. Place a handful of ham and cheese along the length of each sheet, a couple of centimetres in from the edge. Roll tightly. Cut each roll in half and place in a baking dish.

Place the garlic and cream in a large frypan, and stir over medium heat until it comes to a gentle boil. Add the tomatoes, wine, mushrooms and olives. Pour over the pasta rolls and sprinkle with mozzarella. Bake at 180°C for 30 minutes.

Remove from the oven and decorate the top with chopped fresh tomato, flat-leaf parsley and basil.

Butter Chicken in Poppadom Baskets

Serves 4–6

3 double chicken breasts, skin and bones removed
approx. 3 tablespoons tandoori paste (Pataks and Aashiayana are
good brands, or you can use dry tandoori seasoning powder)
2 tablespoons oil
1 tablespoon white wine vinegar
100 g butter
2 onions, chopped roughly
250 g (approx. 3 cups) button mushrooms, sliced
3 medium zucchini, sliced
½ cup chopped parsley
½ cup chopped fresh coriander
500 g (2 cups) sour cream or thick natural yoghurt
extra chopped coriander and parsley, to garnish

Cut the chicken into bite-sized pieces and place in a casserole dish. Mix the tandoori paste with the oil and the white-wine vinegar and stir into the chicken, coating well. Leave covered in the fridge for a couple of hours (at least half an hour, preferably overnight).

When ready to cook, heat the oven to 200°C. Heat the butter in a small pan or in the microwave, and cook the onion to soften. Add the chicken and mix in the mushrooms, zucchini, parsley, coriander and half the sour cream or yoghurt. Bake for about 20 minutes, until the chicken has cooked through. Stir in the remaining sour cream or yoghurt, mix well, and sprinkle over the extra herbs to garnish. (If necessary, it can be thickened with a little cornflour mixed with cold water.)

Serve with rice and naan bread, or in a poppadom basket. The easiest way to make these is by placing a poppadom over a glass or cup in the microwave and cooking for a minute on high. The poppadom folds over the glass to form a basket shape. These will keep crisp in an airtight container.

Pistachio Butter

½ cup shelled pistachios
10 large fresh basil leaves
1–2 cloves garlic, crushed
125 g butter, softened
juice and grated rind of 1 lime

Process the pistachios, basil leaves and garlic in a food processor until finely chopped. Add the butter, juice and grated rind, and process until well mixed. Season to taste with salt and freshly ground black pepper. Transfer the butter mixture to a small bowl. Refrigerate until well chilled (it can be prepared up to 4 days ahead).

Salmon with Pistachio-basil Butter

Serves 6

6 thick salmon fillets (at least as big as a Weetbix)
½ cup dry white wine
extra fresh basil leaves, to garnish

Preheat the oven to 200°C. Grease, or spray with oil, a suitable baking dish and place the salmon fillets in the dish (or on a barbecue grill) in a single layer; pour over the white wine. Season the salmon with salt and freshly ground black pepper and bake until the top is almost opaque — about 10 minutes. Place 2 tablespoons of pistachio butter on top of each salmon fillet and continue baking until they are just opaque in the centre, about another 3 minutes.

Transfer the salmon to plates and garnish with basil. Serve immediately.

Chicken Enchiladas with Salsa Verde

Serves 3-4

4 single chicken breasts, skin and bone removed

1 teaspoon dried oregano

1 teaspoon cumin seeds

salt and freshly ground black pepper

100 ml olive oil

3 medium onions, sliced finely

4 ribs celery, sliced finely

2–3 cloves garlic crushed (1 teaspoon)

8 pieces of sun-dried tomato, chopped

1 cup (5–6) shiitake (or brown button) mushrooms, sliced

3 tablespoons chopped coriander

2 cups grated cheddar-style cheese

2 tablespoons freshly squeezed lemon juice

6–8 flour tortillas

basil leaves, to garnish

Salsa Verde

2 slices white sandwich bread
  (no need to remove crusts)

1 cup loosely packed basil
  leaves

1 cup loosely packed flat-leaf
  parsley

juice and rind of 1 medium
  lemon

salt and freshly ground black
  pepper

100 ml extra virgin olive oil

Place all the ingredients except the olive oil in a food processor and process for 2 minutes, then, with the motor running, pour in the oil. Make ahead of time and store in the fridge.

Cut the chicken into thin, finger-like strips. Place in a bowl with the oregano, cumin, salt and freshly ground black pepper, and toss to coat.

Heat half the olive oil in a large frypan and add the onions, celery and garlic. Cook for 3–4 minutes, add the sun-dried tomatoes and the mushrooms, and cook for a further 3 minutes. Remove the mixture from the pan and set aside.

Heat the remaining oil and stir-fry the chicken for 2–3 minutes until it is cooked through — you may need to do this in 2 or 3 batches to keep it golden and fried, rather than overcrowded and potentially stewed. Mix the cooked chicken with the mushroom mixture, add the chopped coriander, 1½ cups of the cheese, and the lemon juice; season and mix well.

Divide the mixture between the tortillas and roll up. Place seam side down in an oil-sprayed baking dish, then sprinkle with the remaining ½ cup of cheese. Cook at 180°C for 25–30 minutes, until golden and bubbling. Spoon over the salsa verde and garnish with the extra basil leaves.

Tequila, Coconut and Lime-marinated Seafood

Serves 4–6

1 kg fresh firm white fish fillets
juice and grated rind of 6 fresh limes (or lemons)
¼ cup tequila (or white-wine vinegar, or a combination of both)
400 ml coconut cream
approx. 4 cups mixed cooked seafood — I've used peeled and
    cooked prawns and smaller shrimps, smoked mussels, fresh
    poached salmon, poached scallops, cooked crayfish, marinated
    baby octopus, squid, crabsticks, and surimi mix
2 medium red peppers, seeded and finely sliced (approx. 1 cup)
3–4 tablespoons capers
3–4 tablespoons chopped parsley
salt and freshly ground black pepper, lime wedges and fresh
    herbs, to garnish

Remove any skin and bones from the fish and cut it into thin, finger-like strips. Toss with the lime (or lemon) juice and the tequila (or white-wine vinegar), cover and allow to marinate for at least 4 hours in the refrigerator, stirring often.

Drain gently, pressing down on the fish in a colander to remove as much liquid as possible. Stir in the coconut cream and all the other ingredients; season with salt and freshly ground black pepper.

Serve chilled and garnished with extra lime wedges and fresh herbs or watercress. This seafood looks great served on palm or banana leaves for a really tropical look.

Roast Peaches with Sweet Chilli Sauce

6 firm but ripe peaches
1 tablespoon liquid honey
2 tablespoons sweet chilli sauce
2 tablespoons oil

Cut the peaches in half and remove the stones. Mix together the honey, chilli sauce and oil, and brush peach halves with this mixture. Roast at 180°C for 30–40 minutes, until the peaches are softened and golden on top.

Maple- and Apricot-glazed Ham with Chilli Peaches and Spiced Oranges

1 cooked ham
1 cup apricot jam
3 tablespoons pure maple syrup

Buy a cooked ham on the bone with the skin on. Carefully peel back and discard the leathery skin, leaving the layer of ham fat intact. Mix the apricot jam and maple syrup together and brush over the ham so that it is coated well. Place the ham in a large roasting tin and bake in a 160°C oven (fan bake) for about 40 minutes — watch that the glaze doesn't burn. If necessary give it a few minutes on 'Grill' to evenly caramelise the topping. Decorate the bone 'handle' with fresh bay leaves, rosemary twigs and raffia or ribbon.

Spiced Oranges

A wonderful side dish for the Christmas ham or turkey — dried apricots can also be prepared this way.

6 oranges
750 ml white wine vinegar
1 kg sugar
1 cinnamon stick
30 cloves
1 vanilla bean

Slice the oranges thinly and place them in a large saucepan with just enough water to cover them. Bring to the boil and simmer for 5 minutes, then lift them out and set aside.

Add the remaining ingredients to the pan and bring to the boil, stirring occasionally. Return the oranges and simmer for 30 minutes. Lift the oranges out of the syrup and place in sterilised vinegar-proof jars (i.e. with plastic lids). Boil the remaining syrup until it reduces to approximately 1 litre. Pour over the oranges, cover and keep in a cool place for at least 2 weeks.

Waterchestnuts, Mushrooms and Bacon

Makes 20

These make a great accompaniment to a glazed ham, and, placed on fresh bamboo skewers or toothpicks, they are also a delicious nibble to have with drinks before dinner.

20 button mushrooms
20 waterchestnuts (approx. 1 × 110 g can, drained)
10 rashers rindless streaky bacon
garlic salt, to sprinkle

Remove the stalks from the mushrooms and place a drained waterchestnut in each cavity. Wrap half a piece of bacon around each to secure it, and thread onto bamboo skewers. Sprinkle with garlic salt and bake at 180°C for 8–10 minutes, until the bacon is crisp — you may need to turn the skewers during baking.

Asian-style Salmon Kebabs

Serves 4–6

approx. 1 kg of salmon fillet, skinned and boned and cut into 30 cubes

Marinade

½ cup rice vinegar
3 tablespoons toasted sesame oil
1 tablespoon minced or grated fresh ginger
1–2 cloves garlic, crushed (1 small teaspoon)
½ teaspoon wasabi paste
¼ cup light soy sauce

Combine the marinade ingredients in a plastic container or bowl, add the salmon cubes and marinate for at least an hour, turning evenly to coat. Thread the salmon carefully onto soaked wooden or bamboo skewers; reserve the marinade. Cook the salmon (2–3 minutes each side) under the grill or on an oiled barbecue plate, brushing with the marinade and turning often. Serve with rice and extra soy sauce enhanced with a little wasabi.

Bacon-wrapped Chicken Stuffed with Orange-flavoured Prunes

Per person:
1 single chicken breast, boneless but skin on
3 orange-flavoured prunes (Sunsweet Orange)
3 short rashers rindless streaky bacon
salt and freshly ground black pepper
rind and juice of ½ an orange

Remove any bone and cartilage from the chicken breast and cut into 3 strips. Leaving the skin intact (the skin keeps the chicken moist), wrap each strip of chicken around a prune and then wrap the whole thing up in a bacon rasher. Secure by threading onto a metal barbecue skewer. Sprinkle with salt, freshly ground black pepper and the grated rind and juice of half an orange.

Bake in a hot oven (200°C) or grill on the barbecue, turning regularly until the bacon and chicken are evenly crisp and cooked through. If cooking in the oven it will take about 30 minutes. Baste a few times during cooking with the pan drippings and orange juice or, on a barbecue grill, with a little olive oil and extra orange juice. Serve on a bed of orange couscous (see page 49) with a simple orange tandoori sauce.

Orange Tandoori Sauce

Serves 8

500 g sour cream (lite sour cream or thick creamy yoghurt)
3 tablespoons prepared tandoori paste (Pataks, Aashiayana, Sharwoods, etc.)
grated rind of 2 oranges
3 tablespoons chopped parsley
3 tablespoons chopped coriander

Mix all the ingredients together, cover, and chill for at least an hour to allow the flavours to develop.

Orange and Currant Couscous

Serves 8

grated rind and juice of 6 oranges
4 cups water
1 teaspoon salt
3 cups couscous
1 cup currants (or sultanas)
1 tablespoon sweet chilli sauce
½ cup chopped parsley
approx. 1 teaspoon freshly ground black pepper

Place the orange juice and rind, water and salt in a large pan and bring to the boil. Pour in the couscous and turn off the heat, stir in the currants, sweet chilli sauce and parsley. Allow to rest for 2–3 minutes for the liquid to be absorbed, then fluff up with a fork and season to taste with freshly ground black pepper.

Passionfruit Coriander Chicken

Serves 4

pulp of 3–4 juicy ripe passionfruit (approx. ½–¾ cup)
3 tablespoons oil
2 spring onions, finely sliced
3 tablespoons chopped coriander, plus a couple of sprigs, to
* garnish*
4 chicken breasts (or chicken portions), with bones and skin on

Mix together the passionfruit pulp, oil, spring onions and chopped coriander. Marinate the chicken breasts in this for 2–4 hours, covered, in the fridge (overnight is fine).

Grill or barbecue the chicken for 25–30 minutes, turning often and brushing with the marinade until the skin is crisp and the chicken cooked through.

Serve with extra fresh passionfruit and sprigs of coriander to garnish. A simple mixture of fresh yoghurt, sweet chilli sauce, crushed garlic and chopped coriander is a great accompanying sauce to serve with this.

Thai Grilled Fish

Serves 4

4 fish fillets

1 stick of lemon grass (the tender white core only)

1 green chilli, seeds removed (or 1 tablespoon crushed chilli)

½ small onion, chopped (about 2 tablespoons)

1 clove garlic, crushed (½ teaspoon)

2 cm piece of fresh ginger, grated (1 teaspoon crushed ginger)

2 tablespoons chopped coriander stems and leaves

3 tablespoons desiccated or shredded coconut

½ cup coconut cream

1 teaspoon brown sugar

juice and grated rind of a small lime (or lemon)

½ teaspoon salt

½ teaspoon turmeric

6 kaffir lime leaves, finely sliced, to serve (optional)

lime or lemon wedges, to serve

Place each fish fillet on a sheet of tinfoil. Mix all the other ingredients in a food processor or pound in a pestle and mortar to form a thick paste. Spread over the fish and enclose in the tinfoil like a parcel. Place on a baking tray and cook for 20 minutes at 180°C, or place on a barbecue grill and turn after 10 minutes.

To serve, place each parcel on a plate, open it and sprinkle with the chopped kaffir lime leaves, and garnish with lime wedges. This is great with rice.

Gnocchi with Fresh Sage Butter

Serves 4

about 6 medium potatoes, peeled and chopped
1½ cups flour
2 tablespoons olive oil
1 teaspoon salt
1 teaspoon finely ground white pepper

Fresh Sage Butter

125 g butter
1 bunch fresh sage, chopped
freshly ground black pepper

Place the butter and sage in a pan. Cook until the butter has melted and turns a pale brown. Add freshly ground black pepper. Place the gnocchi in soup bowls and pour the sauce over.

Cook the potatoes until tender. Drain, return to the pan and heat for 2 minutes to dry out. Mash to remove any lumps and transfer to a bowl. Add the flour, oil, salt and white pepper, and mix with a wooden spoon to form a soft dough. Turn onto a lightly floured surface and knead gently for about 4 minutes.

Divide the dough into 4 equal pieces. Using floured hands, roll each piece into a sausage 40 cm long. Cut each roll into 2.5 cm pieces. Roll into a smooth ball and indent with a fork.

Lower small batches of gnocchi into a saucepan of boiling water and cook for 2–3 minutes, until the gnocchi rise to the surface. Drain and keep warm.

Gnocchi Know-how

- Always use waxy potatoes — Desirees or Red Rascals.
- Cook potatoes until tender to avoid a lumpy mash. Mash while hot and use when warm to mix easily with the flour.
- To avoid hard gnocchi, don't over-knead. Knead gently until the dough is smooth but still sticky.
- When shaping and indenting the gnocchi use a long-pronged dinner fork and keep dipping it in flour as you go.
- As the gnocchi float to the top of the boiling water remove them with a slotted spoon and let the excess water drain away. If the gnocchi sit in water, they become spongy and fall apart.

Mussels in White Wine with Garlic Cream

Serves 4

2 egg yolks
2 cloves garlic, roughly chopped
1 tablespoon lemon juice
salt and freshly ground black pepper
¾ cup olive oil
½ cup cream
1.5 kg small green-lipped mussels
1 tablespoon oil
1 onion, chopped
3 spring onions, sliced
1 teaspoon bottled or fresh chopped chilli
½ cup white wine
½ cup chopped parsley

To make the garlic cream, place the yolks, garlic, lemon juice, salt and freshly ground black pepper in a food processor and blend until smooth. Gradually add the olive oil in a thin stream while the motor is running. Process until thick and smooth, then transfer to a bowl and stir in the cream.

Remove the beards from the mussels, scrub the outside of the shells and discard any mussels with opened or cracked shells. Heat 1 tablespoon of oil in a large pan, add the onion, spring onions and chilli. Cook, stirring until the onions have softened, then add the mussels and wine. Simmer the mixture (covered) for 3–5 minutes or until the mussels have opened. Stir through the parsley and serve with the pan juices in large bowls. Drizzle with some garlic cream.

Barbecue Lamb with Yoghurt Mint Sauce

Serves 4

This is a great recipe for livening up lamb. The sauce is also good with lamb chops, burgers and lamb sausages. Easy to prepare and a great flavour burst.

Yoghurt Mint Sauce

250 g natural sweetened yoghurt (add a little honey if you only have unsweetened yoghurt)

3 tablespoons chopped fresh mint leaves

3 tablespoons mint sauce

2–3 cloves garlic, crushed (1 teaspoon)

1 tablespoon sweet chilli sauce (or to taste)

freshly ground black pepper

Mix all the ingredients together and serve alongside the barbecue lamb.

approx. 750 g lamb loins, fillets or boned out leg of lamb, cut into 2–3 cm cubes

¼ cup bottled mint sauce (the old-fashioned vinegar style)

¼ cup oil

2–3 cloves garlic, crushed (1 teaspoon)

Mix all the ingredients together, cover, and leave to marinate in the fridge for a couple of hours.

Grill or barbecue the lamb until it is roasty brown outside but still pink and juicy tender inside (depending on the size of the pieces about 7–10 minutes); turn often. Serve with the yoghurt mint sauce and a crisp green salad.

Some Great Little Barbecue Ideas

Halve poussins or little chickens and season with melted butter, garlic and lemon juice. Barbecue for 20–25 minutes, brushing with the melted butter and turning often.

Liven up sausages by brushing with one of the following as they cook:

- Tomato ketchup, grated onion and Worcester sauce.
- Brown sugar, oil, grainy mustard and crushed garlic.
- Fresh lime or lemon juice with sweet chilli sauce.

Use focaccia or ciabatta breads, onion and cheese bagels, or slices of toasted French bread instead of plain burger buns.

Brush lamb fillets, steak or chicken with a spice rub (Kato make two great flavours) or tandoori/curry paste before grilling.

Add a good slosh of alcohol to your salad dressing: tequila, Kahlua, Cointreau, etc. to a basic vinaigrette.

Turkey, Apricot and Hazelnut Pilaf

Serves 4–6

A great brunch dish to use up all that leftover Christmas turkey.

2 tablespoons olive (or hazelnut) oil

10–12 small pickling onions, peeled but left whole

3 cloves garlic, crushed (1 teaspoon)

1 tablespoon mild curry powder

1 teaspoon ground coriander

1 teaspoon mixed spice

3 sticks celery, finely sliced

1 cup plump dried apricots, cut into halves

1 cup brown rice

3 cups chicken stock

salt and freshly ground black pepper

2–3 cups cooked turkey meat (a turkey breast cooked in the microwave or cold roast turkey leftovers)

1 handful trimmed small French green beans

½ cup toasted peeled hazelnuts (roast then roll in a towel and the skins will come off)

½ cup chopped fresh coriander

flat-leaf parsley sprigs, to garnish

Heat the oil in a large pan and stir-fry the onions, garlic, curry powder, ground coriander and mixed spice for 5–10 minutes, until the onions are brown and softened. Add the celery, halved apricots, rice and chicken stock. Bring to the boil, season with salt and freshly ground black pepper and simmer, covered, for about 15 minutes, stirring often. Check whether the rice is tender and the stock has been absorbed; add a little extra stock or water until the rice is cooked.

Shred the turkey and add it to the rice with the green beans, hazelnuts and coriander. Stir for a few more minutes until heated through. Check the seasonings, and garnish with flat-leaf parsley.

Grilled Vegetable Lasagne

Serves 6–8

2 yellow peppers, seeded and sliced into big chunky pieces
2 red peppers, seeded and sliced as above
6 zucchini, sliced lengthways
2 aubergines (eggplants), sliced lengthways
1 red onion, thickly sliced
10 cloves of garlic, peeled
olive oil
6–8 sheets fresh pasta (e.g. Pasta Fresca)
10 large spinach leaves
8–10 large field-type mushrooms, sliced
8 tomatoes (outdoor, Roma are preferable)
approx. 1 cup basil leaves
½ cup chopped parsley
1 cup shaved or coarsely grated parmesan cheese
2 cups grated mozzarella cheese
salt and freshly ground black pepper

Place the peppers, zucchini, aubergines, red onion and garlic on a baking tray, sprinkle with olive oil and grill (or roast) until soft and golden coloured. Oil a large lasagne dish and layer up the lightly cooked sheets of lasagne (i.e. plunged into boiling water to soften) with all the vegetables, cheese and herbs. Generously sprinkle each layer with salt and freshly ground black pepper. Finish with a layer of grated cheeses.

Cook for 40–45 minutes at 160°C.

Mustard Balsamic Chicken on Polenta with Pawpaw Salsa

Serves 4

2 teaspoons crushed garlic
2 tablespoons grainy mustard
2 tablespoons olive oil
3 tablespoons balsamic vinegar
salt and freshly ground black pepper
4 chicken breasts, skin and bone removed
salad leaves, to garnish

Pawpaw Coriander Salsa

1 small pawpaw, halved, seeded and coarsely chopped
2 teaspoons sweet chilli sauce, or finely chopped fresh chilli, to taste
1 small red pepper, diced
1 small red onion, peeled and finely chopped
½ cup finely chopped fresh coriander
3 tablespoons fresh lemon or lime juice
2 tablespoons olive oil
salt and freshly ground black pepper, to taste

Mix all the ingredients together, cover, and chill for at least 1 hour and up to 3 hours. Stir just before serving.

Mix together the garlic, mustard, olive oil, balsamic vinegar, salt and freshly ground black pepper. Pour over the chicken breasts and allow to marinate for at least 10–15 minutes.

Cook the chicken in a preheated frypan, under the grill or on the barbecue for approximately 3–4 minutes each side, until cooked through.

Serve with a wedge of polenta, a dollop of pawpaw coriander salsa, and some salad leaves to garnish.

Parmesan Polenta

4 cups chicken or vegetable stock, or milk
salt and pepper, to taste
1½ cups polenta cornmeal
1 cup grated parmesan cheese

Bring the stock or milk to the boil and add salt and pepper to taste. Pour the polenta into the boiling stock in a steady flow while you stir continuously. Turn down the heat to a very gentle simmer for about 5 minutes. Stir until the polenta is thick and smooth, then stir in the parmesan cheese. Pour into a 20 cm cake tin and allow to set for approximately 30 minutes, then brown under the grill or in a frypan. Cut into wedges to serve.

Cinnamon Maple Pork Kebabs

Serves 4

¼ cup pure maple syrup

1 teaspoon ground cinnamon

1 tablespoon white wine vinegar

1 tablespoon oil

2–3 pork fillets cut into 2–3 cm pieces, or approx. 500 g Trim Pork pieces

fresh or canned pineapple pieces

Mix the maple syrup, cinnamon, white wine vinegar and oil together in a shallow bowl or marinating dish. Toss the pork pieces in the marinade and leave covered in the fridge for 4–6 hours. Thread the pork pieces alternately with fresh or canned pineapple pieces onto metal (or bamboo soaked in water) skewers and grill or barbecue for 5–7 minutes, turning often. Serve with a salad or rice couscous, with a fruity salsa or chutney sauce.

Lamb and Feta Salad with Fresh Basil Dressing

Serves 8

This is the meat and salad course all in one. It travels particularly well, and is in fact better mixed and then eaten a few hours later, allowing the flavours to really develop.

1 kg lamb fillets or lamb loins, boneless leg steaks, or leg of lamb, boned and cut into bite-sized pieces

1–2 tablespoons olive oil

3 cups (approx. 250 g) sliced button mushrooms

2 red peppers, seeded and sliced into strips

2 punnets (approx. 500 g) cherry tomatoes

4–6 medium zucchini, sliced

approx. 150 g feta cheese, cut into cubes

2 cups pitted black olives

½ cup chopped chives or the green stems of spring onions

Dressing

½ cup olive oil

2 tablespoons white wine vinegar

2 cloves garlic, crushed (1 teaspoon)

2 tablespoons chopped fresh basil

2 tablespoons chopped parsley

lots of salt and freshly ground black pepper, to taste (but remember the feta can be quite salty)

Heat the oil in a large pan over high heat (or on the barbecue), and stir-fry the lamb until seared and brown, 3–4 minutes. Remove and cool.

Mix the dressing ingredients in a blender or screw-top jar.

In a large bowl or plastic picnic container, mix the lamb and salad ingredients together, pour over the dressing and toss to mix well. Check seasonings and serve immediately or chill for 2–3 hours to allow the flavours to develop.

Minted Pepper-crusted Lamb with Port and Plum Chutney Sauce

Serves 8

4 lamb loins, about 300 g each
½ cup mint jelly
¼ cup freshly ground black pepper

Plum and Port Chutney

½ cup cranberry sauce
1 × 825 g can plums, drained and chopped
½ cup port
2 tablespoons brown sugar
1 tablespoon fresh rosemary, chopped

Preheat the oven to 180°C. Brush the lamb with mint jelly. Sprinkle the pepper on a sheet of greaseproof paper and roll the lamb evenly in the pepper. Place the lamb in a lightly oiled baking dish and bake for 12–15 minutes; the juices should run pink when tested with a skewer. Stand for 10 minutes before slicing. Serve with plum and port chutney.

To make the chutney, combine all the ingredients in a pan and slowly bring to the boil, stirring until the sugar is dissolved. Reduce to a simmer and cool, uncovered, for 20 minutes or until the mixture thickens. The chutney can be made up to 3 days ahead.

Vegetables, Salads and Side Dishes

Wild-rice Salad

Serves 4–6

2 cups brown rice
1 cup white rice (long grain)
*1 cup wild rice (you may need to buy this as a gourmet blend of
    rice)*
2 tablespoons olive oil
1 large red onion, finely chopped
10 spring onions (2 bunches)
3 ribs or stalks of celery
1 small red pepper, chopped into fine dice
1 cup chopped mixed fresh herbs (chives, parsley, etc.)
½ cup vinaigrette dressing
½ cup pinenuts or other nuts, chopped
salt and freshly ground black pepper, to taste

Cook the rice according to the instructions on the packs —
I generally have a large saucepan of boiling salted water and
start with the brown rice; after 10 minutes I add the long-grain
white rice and the wild rice or gourmet blend. I cook for a further
10 minutes then check the rice to see that the brown and white
rice are soft. The wild rice should be tender but still have quite
a crunchy bite to it. Drain and rinse in cold water, then leave to
cool.

Heat the oil in a medium-sized pan, add the red onion and
spring onions and cook for 2–3 minutes to soften. Cool, then mix
all the rice and the other ingredients together. Check the
seasonings, adding extra salt and lots of freshly ground black
pepper to taste.

This is a good basic recipe that can have all sorts of bits and
pieces added to it — pieces of chicken or sausage, herbs, nuts,
gherkins, diced vegetables, etc.

Pan-fried Cucumber with Sweet Chilli and Mint

Serves 4

The hint of chilli balances the cool mint and gives a good flavour as well as an attractive colour to this dish.

1 large telegraph cucumber
50 g butter
1 tablespoon olive oil
1 teaspoon sweet chilli sauce
salt and freshly ground black pepper
¼ cup finely chopped fresh mint

Peel the cucumber and cut it in half lengthways. Using a teaspoon, scoop out and discard the seeds. Cut each of the two lengths into 1 cm slices.

Melt the butter in a large frypan. Add the oil and chilli sauce. Sauté the cucumber until it has softened and heated through, about 2–3 minutes. Season to taste and sprinkle with the chopped mint. Serve immediately.

Sweet-and-sour Spiced Vegetable Salad

Serves 6–8

3 small zucchini, sliced

3 small yellow scallopini (or yellow zucchini), sliced

1 red pepper, sliced

1 yellow pepper, sliced

1 small cauliflower, broken into florets and blanched in boiling water for 2 minutes

1 small red onion, finely sliced

a handful small sugar-snap peas in the pod, or little French beans, topped and tailed

Marinade

½ cup red-wine vinegar

½ cup sugar

¼ cup olive oil

½ teaspoon salt

1–2 cloves garlic, crushed (1 teaspoon)

2 tablespoons grainy mustard

Place all the vegetables in a large plastic or ceramic container with a tightly fitting lid. In a saucepan combine the vinegar, sugar, oil, salt, garlic and mustard, and bring to the boil. Pour the mixture over the vegetables, place the lid on the container and turn it upside down so that the vegetables are well coated. Leave in the marinade for at least 6 hours (up to 3 days), turning often to mix and coat the vegetables. Drain and serve with chopped herbs — fresh parsley, chives, etc. — to garnish.

Roast Radishes and Onions with Balsamic Vinegar

Serves 6–8

People don't usually think of radishes as a roasting possibility, but they are great. They turn a beautiful pale rose pink colour and in this combination with juicy red onions and sweet balsamic dressing they're just fabulous. This is one of those dishes that looks stunning and is so simple to achieve.

3–4 bunches radishes, trimmed, topped and tailed (about 20 radishes, depending on the size; allow 2–3 per person)

4–6 large red onions, outer papery skins peeled off, cut into 4 or 6 wedges (like a wedge of lemon)

approx. ¼ cup olive oil

salt to sprinkle (I use the Maldon sea salt as I love the flaky texture)

¼ cup balsamic vinegar

Toss the radishes and onion wedges in olive oil and sprinkle with salt. Roast in a hot oven (200°C) for approximately 35–40 minutes, stirring a couple of times, until the onions are crisp and the radishes fairly tender when tested with a sharp knife tip. Sprinkle over the balsamic vinegar and toss to coat well.

Serve as a side dish or as a vegetable dish alongside roast meat. This looks spectacular presented on a big platter.

Peas and Beans with Peanut-butter Sauce

Serves 4

2 handfuls French beans, trimmed
2 handfuls sugar-snap or snow peas, trimmed
any other green veg you like (zucchini, asparagus, scallopini, etc.)

Peanut-butter Sauce

3 tablespoons peanut butter
3 tablespoons light soy sauce
1 teaspoon sweet chilli sauce

Blanch the green vegetables then refresh them in cold water. In a small saucepan, or in the microwave, melt the peanut butter, stir in the soy and chilli sauce and toss the vegetables into this mixture.

Tomato, Olive and Bread Salad

Serves 4–6

A hearty Mediterranean lunchtime salad. Use day-old French or Italian bread, as fresh bread will go soggy.

6–8 firm, sun-ripened, outdoor-type tomatoes
1 stick day-old French or Italian-style bread
½ cup extra virgin olive oil
½ cup white-wine vinegar
1–2 cloves garlic, crushed
salt and freshly ground black pepper
1 cup large black olives, stones removed
2 tablespoons flat-leaf parsley or basil, roughly chopped, to garnish

Cut the tomatoes into wedges and tear or cut the bread into similar sized pieces. Combine the oil, vinegar, garlic, salt and freshly ground black pepper. Place the tomatoes and bread in a bowl with the olives and pour over the dressing. Toss well and allow to stand for at least 10 minutes before serving. Garnish with a sprinkling of chopped herbs.

Simple Crispy Roast Potatoes and Onions

Serves 4–6

Buying gourmet washed potatoes makes this a very quick dish to prepare. Allow 2–3 small potatoes per person — people love these and I never seem to have leftovers.

12–16 small potatoes, scrubbed
2 large onions
2–3 tablespoons extra virgin olive oil
a generous sprinkling of garlic salt
chopped parsley, to garnish

Roughly chop the potatoes into cubes or wedges — the smaller the pieces the quicker they cook. Peel and cut the onions into quarters then eighths (like orange segments). Place the potatoes and onions in a large, shallow baking dish, drizzle with olive oil and sprinkle with garlic salt, tossing to coat evenly. Bake in a hot oven (200°C) until golden and crisp, about 20 minutes. Stir a couple of times during cooking. Sprinkle with chopped parsley to serve.

Country Potatoes

Serves 4

An easy, substantial potato dish, great on its own or as a side dish for meats and chicken.

75 g butter, softened
4–5 large potatoes, peeled and sliced
2 onions, thinly sliced
6 rashers rindless bacon, chopped
2-3 cloves garlic (1 teaspoon)
salt and freshly ground black pepper
1½ cups (1 carton) chicken stock
chopped parsley, to garnish

Spread the butter over the base of a small lasagne or oven-proof dish. Layer the potatoes, onions, bacon, garlic, salt and freshly ground black pepper, and pour over the stock. Cover with a tightly fitting lid or tinfoil and bake at 180°C for 30 minutes. Remove the cover and roast for a further 15–20 minutes, until the potatoes are golden brown. Garnish with chopped parsley.

Baked Zucchini with Parmesan

Serves 4

A great new way to serve zucchini, especially useful during the summer glut. This is a nice side dish or even a first course with tomato salsa.

4–8 zucchini (depending on size), topped and tailed
salt and freshly ground black pepper
finely grated parmesan

Blanch the whole zucchini in boiling salted water for 2 minutes until they are barely tender. Drain and cut in half lengthways. Sprinkle the cut side with salt, freshly ground black pepper and parmesan, and bake in the oven at 220°C for 12–15 minutes, until the parmesan is golden.

Spinach Salad with Sour-cream Dressing

Serves 4

1 package (or a couple of handfuls) fresh spinach, washed and
   dried
1 small onion, sliced into thin rings
6 slices bacon, cooked until crisp then crumbled
1 cup sliced mushrooms
2 eggs, hard-boiled and chopped

Sour-cream Dressing

1 cup sour cream
2 teaspoons lemon juice
1 teaspoon grated onion
white pepper
1 teaspoon Worcester sauce
¼ teaspoon salt
1 teaspoon sugar

Tear up the spinach and toss with the onion, bacon, mushrooms and eggs. Combine the remaining ingredients, blending well, and chill for 30 minutes. Toss with the salad.

Mediterranean Salad

Dressing

2 spring onions, finely chopped

1 teaspoon red-wine vinegar

1 teaspoon clear honey

large pinch mustard powder

2 tablespoons freshly
chopped flat-leaf parsley

1 tablespoon freshly chopped
marjoram

6 tablespoons olive oil

salt and freshly ground black
pepper

Put all the dressing ingredients together in a screw-top jar. Screw on the lid and shake until well emulsified, then drizzle over the fish mixture and toss together gently.

Serves 4–6

4 eggs, hard-boiled

a handful French beans, topped and tailed

2 roasted red peppers (Kato brand, vacuum packed in olive oil)

1 cup pitted black olives

approx. 2 cups cherry tomatoes, halved

approx. 2 cups smoked fish fillets

1 small iceberg or cos lettuce, washed and shaken dry

Peel and quarter the hard-boiled eggs. Blanch the beans for 2 minutes and drain, cutting any large beans in half so that they are easier to eat. In a large bowl carefully mix together the eggs, beans, peppers, olives and tomatoes. Skin and coarsely flake the fish fillets and add to the bowl.

Tear any large lettuce leaves into smaller pieces and arrange in a serving bowl. Spoon over the smoked fish/vegetable mixture.

75

Lemon Coleslaw

Serves 6–8

A variation of the classic coleslaw salad, but there's nothing soggy about this — it is a crunchy, sharp and snappy slaw.

8 cups shredded cabbage (approx. 1 medium cabbage)
1 red pepper, cut into matchstick strips
½ small red onion, finely chopped
1 carrot, chopped
½ cup chopped fresh parsley

Combine the vegetables, season with enough dressing to taste, and serve.

Dressing

½ cup mayonnaise
½ cup sour cream
grated rind and juice of 2 juicy lemons
2 tablespoons Dijon mustard
2 tablespoons olive oil
2 tablespoons sugar
1 tablespoon white-wine vinegar
1 tablespoon prepared horseradish sauce
1 teaspoon celery seeds
salt and freshly ground black pepper

Combine the dressing ingredients in a bowl, whisking to blend. Refrigerate the dressing until cold (it can be prepared 1 day ahead).

Tabbouleh Salad

Serves 4

This salad is great for picnics as it travels so well. It can be prepared the day before if necessary.

1½ cups coarse bulghur wheat (bulgar)

2 cups chopped parsley

½ cup chopped mint leaves

6 spring onions, finely sliced

2 large ripe tomatoes, chopped finely

1 large telegraph cucumber, seeds removed (cut in half lengthways and scoop out with a teaspoon) and finely diced

1 tablespoon sweet chilli sauce

¼ cup olive oil

½ cup freshly squeezed lemon juice

salt and freshly ground black pepper, to taste

Place the bulghur wheat in a bowl and cover with cold water; leave to soak for 30 minutes. Drain through a fine sieve, pressing down with the back of a spoon to squeeze out any excess liquid. Spread on paper towels or a clean tea towel and dry off. Combine all the ingredients and toss gently; serve chilled.

Salad Dressings

Asian-style Dressing

Makes ½ cup

1 tablespoon sesame oil
¼ cup light soy sauce
2 tablespoons fresh lemon or lime juice
2 tablespoons brown sugar
2 red chillies, chopped, or 1 teaspoon
   crushed chilli
1 teaspoon Thai fish sauce

Place all the ingredients in a bowl and mix well. Refrigerate for up to 1 week.

Balsamic Dressing

Makes 1 cup

¼ cup balsamic vinegar
½ cup olive oil
1 teaspoon brown sugar
¼ cup chopped basil leaves
freshly ground black pepper

Mix together in a screw-top jar or a blender. Store in the refrigerator for up to 2 weeks.

Caesar Dressing

Makes 1½ cups

1 cup whole-egg creamy mayonnaise
½ cup sour cream
2 tablespoons wholegrain mustard
½ cup grated parmesan cheese
freshly ground black pepper
4 anchovies, chopped

Mix together in a screw-top jar or a blender. Can be stored in the refrigerator for up to 1 week.

Simple Vinaigrette

Makes 1 cup

½ cup olive oil
¼ cup white-wine vinegar
freshly ground black pepper
salt
2 tablespoons wholegrain mustard

Mix together in a screw-top jar or a blender. Can be stored in the refrigerator for up to 3 weeks.

Desserts

Espresso Cups of Chocolate Cream

Serves 4–8 (depending on the cup size)

300 ml cream
1 × 250 g packet chocolate bits (Nestlé choc bits, choc chips or
*   chopped chocolate)*
3 egg yolks
3 tablespoons liqueur (e.g. Cointreau or Kahlua), vanilla or
*   peppermint essence, or strong sweetened espresso coffee*

Heat the cream until it is just about to boil. Throw everything in a blender and run the machine until the racket stops. Pour into little espresso coffee cups or liqueur glasses and chill for at least 3 hours, preferably overnight.

Variations can be made using white or milk chocolate, and even chocolate peppermint creams or Caramello chocolate.

Chocolate Truffle Loaf with Fresh Raspberry Sauce

Serves 4–6

2 cups cream
3 egg yolks
500 g dark chocolate
½ cup corn syrup (Hansells)
125 g butter
¼ cup icing sugar
1 teaspoon vanilla essence

Line a 12 × 21 cm loaf tin with cling film. Mix ½ cup of the cream with the egg yolks. In a small saucepan over medium heat (or in the microwave), stir the chocolate, corn syrup and butter until smooth and well combined. Add the egg mixture and stir constantly for a further 3 minutes. Cool to room temperature. Beat the remaining cream with the icing sugar and vanilla until soft peaks form. Fold into the chocolate mixture.

Pour into the plastic-lined loaf tin and refrigerate overnight, or chill for 3–4 hours in the freezer. Carefully lift out the loaf and peel off the cling film. Slice with a hot knife, wiping the knife between each slice. Serve with raspberry sauce.

Note: Chocolate truffle loaf can be flavoured with a little liqueur or essence and served with an appropriately flavoured sauce. Some suggestions are:
• Chocolate truffle loaf with peppermint chocolate sauce.
• Mocha loaf with coffee liqueur sauce.
• Grand Marnier- or Cointreau-flavoured loaf with chocolate sauce, garnished with orange or mandarin segments.

Raspberry Sauce

2 cups fresh or thawed frozen raspberries
¼ cup sugar, or to taste
a few perfect whole raspberries, to garnish

Purée the raspberries with the sugar in a food processor or blender. Sieve out the seeds and chill. Garnish with whole raspberries.

Velvet Perfection

Serves 6–8

Always a spectacular dessert that has the chocoholics smiling — a flourless chocolate cake with fresh berry sauce and cream.

200 g dark chocolate, chopped (Energy dark chocolate, melts, etc.)
125 g butter
1 teaspoon vanilla (or other essence)
4 eggs, separated
½ cup sugar
1 cup (125 g) ground almonds
½ cup caster sugar

Melt the chocolate and butter together and mix until smooth and well combined; mix in the vanilla, egg yolks, sugar and ground almonds.

Beat the egg whites until soft peaks form, gradually add the caster sugar and beat until thick and glossy (like meringue). Mix a quarter of this egg-white mixture into the chocolate mixture, then fold in the remainder.

Pour into a paper-lined, well-greased and lightly floured 21 cm spring-form pan and bake at 180°C for 55–60 minutes, until dry and crisp and the centre firm to the touch. Cool in the pan. When cool sprinkle with icing sugar, and serve with fresh berry sauce and cream.

Berry Sauce

Purée 2 cups of your favourite berries (raspberry, blackberry, boysenberry, etc.) in the food processor with icing sugar to taste. If desired sieve out the seeds. Serve 'puddled' around a wedge of cake with whipped cream and whole berries to garnish.

New York-style Baked Cheesecake

Serves 6–8

250 g ricotta cheese
250 g cream cheese
250 g sour cream
1 cup caster sugar
¼ cup cornflour
3 eggs
1 teaspoon lemon juice

Grease the sides, and paper line the base of a 20 cm spring-form pan. Place all the ingredients in a food processor and run the machine until the mixture is smooth and creamy. Pour the mixture into the pan and bake at 160°C for an hour. Cool in the pan on a wire rack. Remove from the pan when cool and serve with strawberries and softly whipped cream.

Easy One-mix Ice Cream

Serves 4–6

Ideal for when you don't have the luxury of an ice-cream machine.

1 × 400 g can sweetened condensed milk
3 eggs, separated
1 teaspoon vanilla essence
300 ml cream

Beat the condensed milk, egg yolks and vanilla essence for 3 minutes. Whip the cream until thick and whisk the egg whites until very stiff. Fold all three mixtures together, pour into a chilled container and freeze. This doesn't need any further beating after it freezes.

Variations

- Omit the vanilla essence and add the freshly squeezed juice and grated rind of oranges or lemons.
- Add strawberry essence instead of vanilla, and puréed strawberries. Don't add whole strawberries as they freeze solid like bullets.
- Replace the vanilla essence with coffee essence or strong espresso coffee and for texture add chopped walnuts or chocolate raisins, or chocolate-covered coffee beans.
- Add mashed bananas and toasted coconut with Irish cream liqueur or a few drops of coconut essence.

Christmas Nut Pies

Makes 16

A lovely nutty Christmas version of my now-famous baby pecan pie recipe.

125 g butter

1 cup flour

½ cup icing sugar

1 cup mixed macadamias, hazelnuts (skins removed), pecans and blanched almonds, roughly chopped so nuts are at least cut in half

60 g butter, melted

1 egg

1 cup brown sugar

1 teaspoon vanilla essence

Place the 125 g butter, the flour and icing sugar in a food processor and run the machine until the pastry clumps together in a ball around the blade. Divide into 16 balls and with floured hands press the pastry into the bases and up the sides of non-stick (or well-greased) mini-muffin tins. Refrigerate for at least 30 minutes; the pastry will set quite firm, and you bake it cold like this.

Divide the nuts between the chilled pastry cases. Mix the melted butter, egg, brown sugar and vanilla together until smooth and 'gluey', and spoon or pour carefully over the nuts. Do not overfill each little pie.

Bake in a preheated oven at 180°C for 20–25 minutes, until the pastry is golden brown and the filling puffed and crisp. Take out of the oven and leave in the mini-muffin tins for a few minutes until they are cool enough to handle. Give each pie a little twist around to loosen the bottom, then carefully lift them out to cool completely on a wire rack. They are delicious served warm and can be reheated easily and served with whipped cream or ice cream.

Wicked Chocolate Fudge Brownie

Serves 6–8

375 g dark chocolate (1 packet Nestlé chocolate melts)
200 g butter
2 cups sugar
3 eggs
1 teaspoon vanilla essence
1 cup flour
1 cup nuts

Chocolate Fudge Sauce

375 g dark chocolate (1 packet Nestlé chocolate melts)
300 ml cream
1–2 tablespoons liqueur of your choice (Grand Marnier, Brandy, etc.)

Stir over gentle heat (or microwave) until melted and smoothly combined.

Melt the chocolate and butter together. In a food processor mix the chocolate/butter mixture, the sugar, eggs and vanilla essence until smooth. Mix in the flour and nuts and process until coarsely chopped. Pour into a lined 20 × 30 cm sponge-roll tin and bake at 180°C for 35 minutes.

Cool in the tin for at least 20 minutes before removing. Cut into wedges (or fancy shapes, hearts, etc.) and serve with chocolate fudge sauce and whipped cream.

Butterscotch Meringues

Makes a large platter of piled-up meringues or a generous pavlova that will easily serve 6.

6 egg whites (at room temperature)
2 cups caster sugar
1 teaspoon butterscotch, caramel or vanilla essence
1 teaspoon malt vinegar
2 teaspoons cornflour
whipped cream, to decorate

In a large metal, porcelain or glass bowl (i.e. not plastic) beat the egg whites until soft peaks form. A hand-held electric mixer is ideal for the job.

Gradually, a teaspoon at a time, add the caster sugar. (I emphasise, add the sugar slowly.) The mixture should be getting glossy, thick and shiny with each addition, and the whole sugar-adding process should take about 10 minutes. Beat in the essence, vinegar and cornflour.

Spoon the mixture out into little 'blobs' onto a paper-covered baking tray (or tip out in a large circle for a pavlova).

Bake in a low 110–120°C oven for approximately 45 minutes for individual meringues or 1½ hours for a pavlova. The meringue should be crisp and dry, and easily lift off the baking paper. Cool on a wire rack and decorate with whipped cream when cold.

Baby Pavlovas

Make larger circles of meringue using a small coffee saucer as your guide. They will take the same time to cook as meringues, and they are ready when they feel crisp and dry, and easily lift off the baking paper. When cool top with whipped cream, fresh fruit, praline, mint leaves and chocolate, etc.

Praline

¾ cup sugar

¼ cup water

1 cup nuts (toasted and husked)

Oil-spray a piece of tinfoil or baking paper on a baking tray. Combine the sugar and water in a medium-heavy saucepan and stir over low heat to dissolve the sugar. Increase the heat and boil *without* stirring, until golden. Occasionally brush down the sides of the saucepan with a wet pastry bush and swirl the pan around. Add the nuts and carefully pour the hot praline onto the prepared tray. Cool until the praline hardens, then break into pieces, using a rolling pin to crush. Store in an airtight container.

Meringue Stars

Scoop the basic butterscotch meringue mixture into a piping bag with a round nozzle or just use a small plastic bag and pipe stars, initials or fancy shapes onto a paper-lined baking tray. Cook as for meringues, but these shapes will probably cook fairly quickly (30–35 minutes). When they feel crisp and dry, and lift off the paper easily, they are ready. Cool on a wire rack and store in an airtight container.

Opposite: Baby pavlova with praline

Right: Meringue stars

Espresso Meringues with Chocolate Coffee Sauce

Makes 8–12

Serve these meringues jammed together with whipped cream like a sandwich and drizzled with chocolate coffee sauce.

3 egg whites (at room temperature)
1 cup caster sugar
1 tablespoon sweetened coffee essence, strong black coffee/espresso
½ teaspoon malt vinegar
1 teaspoon cornflour

Make the meringues using the same method as for Butterscotch Meringues (page 91). Bake at 110–120°C for about 45 minutes, until the meringues are crisp and dry and lift easily off the baking paper. Cool on a wire rack.

Whipped Cream

300 ml cream
2 tablespoons sweetened coffee essence, strong sweetened espresso coffee or coffee liqueur (Kahlua, Tia Maria, etc.)

Whip the cream, fold in the coffee essence, espresso or liqueur, and fill the meringues.

Chocolate Coffee Sauce

300 ml cream
375 g dark chocolate (1 packet dark chocolate melts)
3 tablespoons coffee essence (or similar)

In a small saucepan, or in the microwave, melt all the ingredients together and stir until smooth. Pour the sauce over the meringue 'sandwich'. The sauce sets solid when refrigerated, so serve warm.

Instant Soft Fruit Ice Cream

2 cups strawberries, hulled, cut in half and free-flow frozen
   (whole)
¼ cup caster sugar
½ cup cream

Mince the frozen berries in a food processor (don't mind the noise). Add the sugar and briefly process. With the motor on, pour the cream into the mixture through the feed tube. Serve immediately (it loses texture if refrozen).

Variations
- Substitute thick yoghurt for the cream.
- Peaches — peel and cut up before freezing.
- Bananas — freeze in their skins, then peel and slice.
- Blueberries — freeze whole (free-flow).

Quick and Easy Summer Dessert Ideas

Strawberry Drambuie crunch sundaes

Fresh Peaches and Soft Blue Cheese

Serve fresh peaches and soft blue cheese for a delicious simple dessert idea.

Vanilla Poached Apricots

Apricot halves poached in sugar syrup (1 cup water to ¼ cup caster sugar), flavoured with a split vanilla pod (or a little vanilla essence) and served with thick, creamy apricot yoghurt.

Simple Gingered Fruit

For a fabulous speedy dessert slice strawberries, melons and kiwifruit, mix together and serve in melon halves with the seeds scooped out; drizzle with green ginger wine. You can add any other fruits you like, and if desired serve with a creamy fruit yoghurt or fromage frais.

Strawberry Drambuie Crunch Sundaes

In tall parfait glasses, layer sliced ripe strawberries, softly whipped cream, strawberry or rich vanilla ice cream, a splash of liqueur (Drambuie, Cointreau or Grand Marnier). Add broken up meringues (see page 91) or use a packet of store-bought meringue cases. Garnish with a perfect strawberry and fresh mint sprigs.

Fresh fruit kebabs

Strawberries in Balsamic Vinegar

Top and tail ripe strawberries, sprinkle with brown sugar and balsamic vinegar. Toss to coat well and leave for at least 20 minutes. Pile into bowls or tall parfait glasses and serve with whipped cream, yoghurt or ice cream.

Fresh Fruit Kebabs with Orange Cream

Thread pieces of fresh fruit onto bamboo skewers — you can also add pink and white marshmallows and sprigs of mint. The skewers are easy to handle, the fruit doesn't get all mushy and the presentation is spectacular. Serve with orange cream.

Orange Cream

150 ml cream, lightly whipped

150 g sour cream or softened cream cheese

1 teaspoon finely grated orange rind

¼ cup icing sugar

2 teaspoons orange liqueur or fresh orange juice

In a food processor or bowl beat together all the ingredients until smooth. Serve as a sauce or dip for fresh fruit.

Toffee Strawberries

Makes 36

1 cup caster sugar

¼ cup water

approx. 36 strawberries

Dissolve the sugar in the water in a small, heavy saucepan, and boil without stirring — just swirl the pan around until the sugar syrup turns a golden caramel colour. Remove from the heat and dip the strawberries into the syrup, holding them by the stalk. Leave to harden on non-stick baking paper. This also works well with cherries.

New Zealand-style Ice-cream Christmas Pudding

Serves 6–8

A lovely cool New Zealand summer alternative to the steaming Christmas Pudding. You can still serve the traditional custard sauce, but try this for a clever cheat — equal quantities of whipped cream and store-bought custard, with a generous slosh of Irish cream liqueur (Baileys or Carolans or our sneaky homemade version on page 126).

½ cup sultanas
½ cup currants
½ cup chopped raisins
¼ cup finely chopped dessert figs
½ cup brandy
1 packet each of red and green cherries
10 plump dried apricots, chopped
2 litres good quality vanilla ice cream, softened
50 g dark chocolate, chopped (a small chocolate bar)
½ cup flaked almonds, toasted

Combine the sultanas, currants, raisins and figs. Add the brandy and dried fruits, cover, and soak for 12–24 hours, stirring occasionally. Mix the soaked fruits, ice cream, chocolate and almonds together. Line a large pudding bowl, basin or loaf pan with plastic wrap so that it hangs well over the sides. Spoon the mixture into the container, smooth the surface and cover with the overhanging sides of plastic wrap. Freeze until firm. To serve, turn onto a chilled serving platter and surround with seasonal berries.

This pudding can be made in advance and stored for up to 6 weeks in the freezer.

Baking

Lemon Butterfinger Loaf

Serves 6–8

This is great served with fresh fruit and cream as an easy dessert.

¾ cup caster sugar
grated rind of 2 lemons
125 g butter
2 eggs
½ cup milk
1¾ cups self-raising flour

Syrup

juice of 2 lemons
3 tablespoons caster sugar

Mix the caster sugar and grated lemon rind together in the food processor. Add the butter and mix until creamy, then add the eggs, milk and flour.

Line a 12 × 21 cm tin with baking paper, running the paper down one end, along the bottom and up the other end (leave overhangs). Grease the tin and pour in the mixture. Bake at 180°C for an hour, until the loaf shrinks from the sides of the tin.

While the loaf bakes, mix the lemon juice with the 3 tablespoons of caster sugar. As soon as you remove the loaf from the oven, drizzle this mixture over its surface. Remove the loaf from the tin by lifting the paper, and cool on a wire rack. Serve with fresh lemon curd.

Lemon Curd

4 large, juicy lemons
4 eggs, beaten
2 cups sugar
100 g butter

This quantity makes 3 × 250g jars. For a variation, replace the lemons with limes, oranges or tangelos, or passionfruit pulp.

Wash the lemons then finely grate the rind and squeeze the juice into a small saucepan. Add the beaten eggs, sugar and butter cut up into little cubes.

Stir constantly with a wire whisk over very gentle heat until the sugar dissolves and the mixture thickens; keep the heat very low and don't be tempted to speed it up or to stop stirring.

Pour into clean, sterilised hot jars and seal; keep in the fridge.

Rich Christmas Fruit Cake with Brandy-butter Frosting

1.5 kg mixed fruit
250 g glacé cherries, red and green
100 g mixed peel
1 tablespoon grated orange rind
1 tablespoon grated lemon rind
2 tablespoons lemon juice
½ cup brandy
500 g butter
1½ cups brown sugar
8 eggs
2 bananas
1 teaspoon vanilla
4 cups flour
1 cup self-raising flour

Place the mixed fruit, cherries, mixed peel, orange rind, lemon rind, lemon juice and brandy in a large bowl and mix well. Cover and leave overnight.

Cream the butter and sugar until it is light and fluffy, add the eggs one at a time, beating well after each addition, then add the bananas and vanilla. Stir in the fruit mixture, mix well, and add the flour. Mix until well combined.

Place in a deep 25 cm cake tin which had been lined with two thicknesses of brown paper and one thickness of greaseproof paper. Bake in a slow oven (150°C) for approximately 3½ hours, or until a skewer inserted into the middle of the cake comes out clean. I like to ice my cake with brandy-butter frosting.

Brandy-butter Frosting

250 g butter, softened
½ cup brandy
3–3½ cups icing sugar

Beat the softened butter, brandy and 3 cups of icing sugar together, adding extra icing sugar to achieve a smooth spreading consistency. Spread lavishly over the top and sides of the cake, using a palette knife to swirl the frosting into decorative peaks.

Farmhouse Sultana Cake

You always need one of these in the tins over the holidays — perfect for afternoon tea.

500 g sultanas
¼ cup brandy or whisky
250 g butter
1 cup sugar
5 eggs
2½ cups flour
1 teaspoon baking powder
¼ teaspoon salt
1 teaspoon vanilla

Put the sultanas in a saucepan, cover with cold water and bring to the boil. Simmer for 5 minutes then drain. Place the sultanas in a bowl and pour over the brandy or whisky. Leave to cool.

Cream the butter and sugar until light and fluffy. Add the eggs one at a time, beating well after each addition. Sift the flour, baking powder and salt into a bowl.

Add the sultana mixture and the vanilla to the egg mixture, and combine. Add the sifted flour, folding it into the egg mixture.

Pour into a greased and lined 20 cm square cake tin. Bake at 160°C for 1½ hours, or until a skewer inserted into the middle of the cake comes out clean.

Panforte

¾ cup flour

½ cup cocoa

1 teaspoon ground cinnamon

1 cup blanched whole almonds

1 cup walnut halves

1 cup toasted hazelnuts, skins removed

½ cup mixed peel

1 teaspoon finely grated orange rind

1 teaspoon finely grated lemon rind

½ cup caster sugar

¾ cup honey

½ cup icing sugar, for dusting

Preheat the oven to 160°C. Brush a shallow 20 cm round cake tin with oil. Line the base with paper and grease the paper. Place the flour, cocoa and cinnamon in a large mixing bowl. Add the nuts, peel and rind, and stir to combine. Place the sugar and honey in a small, heavy-based pan and stir over low heat until the mixture boils and the sugar has dissolved. Reduce the heat and simmer, uncovered, without stirring for 5 minutes or until the syrup forms a soft ball when a few drops are placed in a glass of cold water.

Pour the hot syrup onto the nut and flour mixture, and stir well to combine. Spoon the mixture into the prepared tin and spread quickly and evenly; bake for 30 minutes, remove from the oven and leave to cool in the tin. When it is completely cool, turn the panforte out onto aluminium foil and wrap well. Leave for 1–2 days before cutting. Dust heavily with icing sugar before cutting into thin wedges.

Blueberry Cinnamon Macadamia Cake

150 g butter, melted
1 cup sugar
2 eggs
2 cups flour
2 teaspoons baking powder
2 teaspoons cinnamon
1 cup chopped macadamias
2 cups fresh or frozen blueberries (there is no reason to defrost)

Mix all the ingredients together and spoon into a well-greased 20–23 cm paper-lined cake tin. Bake at 160°C (fan bake) for 40–45 minutes, or until golden and well cooked in the centre. The cake is done when a skewer inserted in the centre comes out clean. Cool on a wire rack. Serve warm, sprinkled with icing sugar.

Spice Biscuits
Makes 36

A great biscuit for gifts — those hard-to-buy-for people love a homemade bickie. These are quick and easy, and the recipe makes a decent big batch — we always have these in the biscuit tins over the holidays.

250 g butter
1½ cups sugar
1 egg
1 tablespoon golden syrup
2 cups flour
1 teaspoon baking powder
2 teaspoons mixed spice

Beat the butter and sugar until creamy, add the egg and golden syrup, then mix in the dry ingredients. Roll teaspoonfuls of the mixture into little balls and place on greased or non-stick oven trays. Flatten with a wet fork. Bake at 180°C for 12–15 minutes, until golden brown. Cool on a wire rack. Store in an airtight container.

Fresh Nectarine Cake

This recipe works well with fresh apricots, peaches, apples or plums. Great for afternoon tea or as a special dessert.

Serves 6–8 as dessert

200 g butter, softened
1 cup sugar
3 eggs
150 g yoghurt (apricot or peach flavours are great, or just plain)
3 cups fresh nectarines, thinly sliced
½ cup chopped nuts (optional)
juice and grated rind of 1 lemon
2 cups flour
3 teaspoons baking powder
1 teaspoon ground cinnamon

Mix the butter and sugar together in a food processor or large bowl until creamy. Add the eggs and mix well. Mix in the yoghurt, fruit, nuts, lemon juice and rind, flour, baking powder and cinnamon — don't overmix, just mix it until the ingredients are loosely combined. Pour into a well-greased and baking paper-lined 20 cm cake pan. Bake at 180°C for 55–60 minutes; cool on a wire rack. Serve dusted with icing sugar, and accompanied by ice cream or softly whipped cream.

Walnut Kisses

Makes 30

2 egg whites
½ cup sugar
1 teaspoon vanilla
½ cup walnuts, chopped
1 cup cornflakes

Beat the egg whites until frothy. Add the sugar a little at a time, beating well after each addition. Add the vanilla, then mix in the walnuts and cornflakes.

Drop spoonfuls onto an oven tray lined with baking paper, and bake for 25–30 minutes at 180°C (fan bake). Cool on the tray for 10 minutes then transfer to a wire rack to cool completely.

Baked Cinnamon Peach French Toast

Serves 4

Great for brunch, lazy weekend breakfast or as a speedy dessert.

100 g butter, melted
½ cup brown sugar
1 × 425 g can peaches, drained (or canned apricots, apples, pears, etc.)
250 g cream cheese
4 slices toast bread, white or light wholemeal, crusts removed
4 eggs
600 ml milk
2 teaspoons vanilla
1 teaspoon cinnamon

In a medium-sized pie dish (or small lasagne dish), about 20 × 20 cm, mix the melted butter, brown sugar and drained peaches. Cut the cream cheese into cubes or teaspoonfuls and place evenly over the peaches. Cut the bread in half diagonally to form triangles, and layer over the peaches.

In a bowl beat together the eggs, milk and vanilla. Pour the egg mixture over the bread, making sure that all the bread is dampened. Sprinkle with cinnamon.

Bake for 35–40 minutes at 180°C, until golden and puffed. Stand for 10 minutes before serving. This reheats well if you are serving it as a dessert; accompany the French toast with whipped cream and ice cream.

Angel Food Cake

Serves 8–10

A spectacular dessert cake, absolutely low, low fat — which of course you can change by serving it with lashings of whipped cream or rich ice cream, if you want. You need a special angel food cake tin (or tube tin) to cook this cake, but you'll love it as I do, so it will be a good investment!

1 cup flour
1½ cups sugar
12 egg whites
½ teaspoon cream of tartar
2 teaspoons vanilla essence
2 teaspoons grated lemon rind
berries, to accompany

Sift the flour and half the sugar into a bowl and set aside. Place the egg whites and cream of tartar in a bowl and beat until soft peaks form. Gradually add the remaining sugar to the egg whites, and beat until they are thick and glossy.

Fold the vanilla, lemon rind and the flour mixture into the egg whites. Pour the mixture into a *non-greased* 23 cm angel food cake tin and bake at 190°C for 35–40 minutes, or until the cake is cooked when tested with a skewer. Invert the tin and allow the cake to cool, then run a knife around the edges of the tin to release the cake. Serve with mixed berries and whipped cream.

Christmas Decoration Biscuits

Makes 36

250 g butter
½ cup caster sugar
1 teaspoon vanilla
2¾ cups flour
3 tablespoons cocoa
½ cup chopped boiled sweeties (e.g. Lifesavers)

In the food processor mix the butter, sugar and vanilla, then add the flour and cocoa. Roll out to about 8 mm (nearly a centimetre) thick, and cut out Christmas shapes — stars, trees, etc. Place on a baking tray lined with baking paper or teflon sheet, and chill for at least half an hour. With a little cutter, cut a hole in the middle of each.

Bake for 10 minutes at 150°C then remove from the oven and fill the centre hole with chopped sweeties. Turn the oven up to 180°C and bake for a further 10 minutes, until the sweeties have melted and the biscuits have cooked. Cool on the tray.

Shortbread Stars

Makes 24

250 g butter, softened
¾ cup icing sugar
½ cup cornflour
1½ cups flour

Beat the butter and icing sugar until creamy. Mix in the cornflour and flour. On a floured surface roll out the dough to a thickness of 1 cm, and press out star shapes. Carefully place on a greased oven tray, or a tray lined with baking paper. Prick with a fork. Bake at 150°C for 25–30 minutes, until the shortbread is pale but crisp. Cool on a wire rack and store in an airtight container.

Coconut Pecan Biscotti

Makes 36

A wonderful treat to dunk into dessert wine or coffee — these make a lovely present.

1 egg and 1 extra egg white
½ cup soya oil
¾ cup sugar
1 teaspoon vanilla
1 cup chopped pecans
½ cup coconut
1½ cups flour
2 teaspoons baking powder
½ teaspoon salt

In a food processor mix the egg, egg white and oil until well blended. Add the sugar, vanilla, pecans and coconut, and mix until just blended. Add the flour, baking powder and salt. Form into two logs, wrap in plastic film and chill for at least an hour (I usually do this in the freezer). Place the logs on a paper-covered oven tray and bake at 160°C for 40 minutes. The logs should be lightly browned and have fluffed out. Cool slightly until you can handle them with ease, then cut each log into 1.5 cm slices; lay these on their side (like toast to be buttered) on the paper-lined oven tray. Bake for a further 15–20 minutes, until the cut sides are golden brown. Cool on a wire rack.

Featherweight Cheese Puffs

Makes about 12

3 cups grated cheese
2 cups flour
4 teaspoons baking powder
2 eggs
¾ cup milk

Preheat the oven to 240°C (the hottest it will heat to). Mix all the ingredients together in a large bowl. Drop spoonfuls of mixture onto a well-greased or non-stick oven tray and place in the hot oven immediately. Make sure you close the oven door as quickly as possible, then turn the oven off. Bake for 10 minutes. Remove from the oven and cool on a wire rack. Serve warm.

Quick Onion Yoghurt Bread

3 cups self-raising flour
1 packet dried onion soup mix
2 cups plain natural yoghurt (or buttermilk)
1 tablespoon milk, to brush top

Grease a 14 × 21 cm loaf pan. Mix together the self-raising flour and the onion soup mix. Add the yoghurt and mix to a soft, sticky dough. Place in the loaf tin and brush the top with milk. Bake for an hour at 180°C. Cool on a wire rack.

Beer Bread

This is one of my signature recipes, and I couldn't possibly leave it out. It's a wonderfully quick bread that has the texture, taste and — best of all — the smell of a lovely fresh-from-the-oven farmhouse loaf.

3 cups flour

3 teaspoons baking powder

1 teaspoon salt

1 can beer (approx. 400 ml; just rinse out the can with water to make up the volume); don't use low-alcohol beer

1 handful (about ½ cup) grated cheese

Preheat the oven to 200°C. Mix the flour, baking powder, salt and beer in a large bowl until well combined. Tip into a large 12 × 21 cm non-stick or well-greased loaf tin, or two 8 × 15 cm tins. Sprinkle the top with grated cheese.

Bake the large loaf for 50–60 minutes, the two smaller loaves for 30–40 minutes, until golden brown.

Tip out and cool on a wire rack before slicing. This bread keeps well and also makes excellent toast.

Waffles

Makes 8

2 cups self-raising flour

2 tablespoons caster sugar

3 eggs, separated

1½ cups milk

100 g butter, melted

1 teaspoon vanilla

extra butter for greasing waffle iron

Sift the flour and sugar into a bowl. Mix in the egg yolks, milk, melted butter and vanilla. Mix to a smooth batter.

In a separate bowl beat the egg whites until stiff peaks form, then fold carefully into the batter.

Brush a heated waffle iron with melted butter, spoon in 2–3 tablespoons of batter and cook until the waffles are crisp and golden brown. Serve warm with whipped cream and maple syrup.

For a variation, add ½ teaspoon mixed spice to the batter and serve with poached apple slices and cinnamon cream or honey.

Toasted Cheese Muffins

Makes 12

2 cups flour
4 teaspoons baking powder
½ teaspoon salt
1 cup grated tasty cheese
1 egg
¼ cup oil
1¼ cups milk

Stir all the ingredients together in a large bowl, lightly mixing to combine. Don't overwork the mixture or the muffins will be tough and heavy. Spoon the mixture, which should be fairly runny and pourable, into deep, greased muffin tins. Sprinkle a few shreds of grated cheese over the top. Bake in a hot oven (200°C) for 15–20 minutes, until golden brown.

Variations

To make savoury muffins, add any of the following to the toasted cheese muffin recipe: chopped herbs, finely sliced spring onions, nuts, a tablespoon of fruit chutney or relish, chopped pickled onions or gherkins, crumbled blue cheese, chopped ginger or crushed garlic.

Blueberry Muffins

Makes 12

1 teaspoon baking powder
2 cups self-raising flour
½ cup caster sugar
1 cup milk
100 g butter, melted
2 eggs, lightly beaten
1 cup blueberries (if using frozen, don't thaw)
grated rind and juice of a lemon

Mix all the ingredients in a large bowl until just combined — don't overmix.

Grease or oil-spray deep muffin tins, spoon in the mixture and bake at 200°C for 12–15 minutes. Cool on a wire rack and serve buttered and dusted with icing sugar.

Special Drinks and After-dinner Treats

White Christmas

Makes 36 pieces

2½ cups Rice Bubbles
1 cup coconut
¾ cup icing sugar
1 cup full cream milk powder
1 cup mixed dried fruit (fruit cake mixture)
½ cup each red and green glazed cherries (approx. 100 g each)
250 g solid vegetable shortening (Kremelta), melted

Place all the ingredients together in a large bowl and mix well. Press into a 20 × 30 sponge-roll pan. Refrigerate and cut into squares, diamonds, or even Christmas shapes when cold.

Russian Fudge

Makes 36 pieces

3½ cups sugar
125 g butter
3 tablespoons golden syrup
½ cup milk
½ teaspoon salt
200 g sweetened condensed milk (½ the standard 400g can)
2 teaspoons vanilla essence

Place all the ingredients *except* the vanilla into a medium-heavy saucepan. Warm over a gentle heat until the sugar has dissolved. Bring to a gentle boil and cook for about 15–20 minutes, until it reaches the soft ball stage (120°C).

Remove from the heat and add the vanilla. Beat (I use an electric mixer) until the fudge is creamy and thick and has lost its gloss. Pour into a greased 20 cm cake pan. Score the top and break into pieces when cold.

Chocolate Pecan Fudge

Makes 36 pieces

*3 cups chocolate chips or roughly chopped dark chocolate
(375–400 g)*
1 × 400 g can condensed milk
1 cup pecans
*2 teaspoons vanilla essence (or orange essence, orange liqueur,
etc.)*

Melt the chocolate and condensed milk together in a heavy saucepan over low heat (or microwave in a large bowl); stir until smooth. Remove from the heat and stir in the pecans and vanilla. Spread evenly into a tinfoil-lined 20–23 cm square pan. Chill for at least 2 hours, until really firm. Cut with a warm knife.

Honey Walnut Fudge

Makes 36 pieces

1½ cups sugar
1 cup brown sugar
1 cup cream
2 tablespoons honey
50 g butter
1 teaspoon vanilla
1 teaspoon finely grated orange peel
½ cup chopped walnuts

Line a 20-cm-square tin with foil and spray with oil. Spray the sides of a medium-heavy saucepan with oil. Place the sugar, brown sugar, cream and honey in the saucepan and stir over a medium to high heat, bringing the mixture to the boil. At the soft ball stage (120°C, using a sugar thermometer to check) remove from the heat, add the butter, vanilla and orange peel — do not stir, but cool until 70°C then beat until it starts to thicken. Add the nuts and continue to beat until the fudge starts to lose its gloss and is very thick, then pour into the prepared pan. Score into squares while still warm — if desired press a walnut half into each square.

White Chocolate Cointreau Fudge Truffles

Makes 50

375 g dark chocolate (1 packet Nestlé chocolate melts)
200 g butter
150 g mixed peel
¼ cup Cointreau (or other orange liqueur) or orange juice
grated zest of 1 orange (about 1 teaspoon)
3 cups icing sugar
750 g white chocolate for dipping (2 packets Nestlé chocolate melts)

Variations

- For cappuccino truffles replace the Cointreau with coffee liqueur or essence and omit the mixed peel and grated orange rind. These can be dipped in white or dark chocolate.
- For peppermint truffles omit the Cointreau, mixed peel and orange rind, and add 1–2 teaspoons of peppermint essence.
- For toasted coconut and liqueur truffles, replace the Cointreau, mixed peel and orange rind with Irish cream liqueur or Baileys, etc., and add ½ cup toasted coconut.

Melt the dark chocolate and butter together in the microwave on medium heat for about 4 minutes, stirring a couple of times during cooking. Stir in the mixed peel, Cointreau, orange zest and icing sugar until well combined. Chill in the fridge until firm enough to handle and roll into balls about the size of a walnut.

Place the balls on a foil-lined tray and freeze until really solid — about 2 hours. Melt the white chocolate in the microwave on medium power or over a pot of hot water, and dip the truffles in the melted chocolate. A chocolate dipping fork, available at good cookware shops, is invaluable for this job. Allow the excess chocolate to drip off, and leave to set on a foil-covered tray.

Do not store in the fridge as the chocolate tends to sweat, but keep them in a cool place. A good idea is to keep a plastic container of undipped truffles in the freezer, to be removed and dipped as you need them, for after-dinner treats or small gifts.

119

Coffee Granita

Serves 6

Granita is a rough-textured sorbet made from coffee or fruit-flavoured syrup, frozen to form fine ice crystals. Coffee granita is served in every café and coffee bar in Italy during the hot summer months. It is made with espresso coffee and served topped with a spoonful of whipped cream, and dusted with cocoa powder or freshly ground espresso beans.

300 ml strong espresso coffee
½ cup caster sugar
75 ml Tia Maria or other coffee liqueur
1 cup cream
1 level tablespoon icing sugar
cocoa powder, to dust

Mix together the warm coffee, caster sugar and 45 ml of the Tia Maria, and stir until all the sugar has dissolved. Pour into a shallow freezer container and freeze overnight. Next morning, mash with a fork to break up the ice crystals. The granita should have a rough texture. Return it to the freezer until ready to serve.

Lightly whip the cream, stir in the remaining Tia Maria and the icing sugar, then cover and chill until required.

To serve, break up the granita and spoon it into 6 glasses. Top with spoonfuls of the cream, and dust with cocoa powder. Serve immediately as the granita will melt very quickly.

Old-fashioned Lemon Drink

Makes 3 litres of lemon cordial

This is my dear friend Heather's lemon drink and she knows her lemons. She lives on a lemon orchard in Clevedon and people drive for miles to buy her Villa Franca lemons from the gate stall. This is the most refreshing drink I know — great after a blast in the garden or on the tennis court, and equally good served hot with a shot of whisky for a winter cure-all.

6 lemons
1.5 kg sugar
50 g (½ packet) citric acid
boiling water

Peel the rind off 2 of the lemons, taking care to get just the outer skin, no white pith (use a potato peeler).

Place the peel and 2 cups of the sugar in the food processor and run the processor until the rind is really ground up and the sugar is yellow and oily looking.

Squeeze all 6 lemons and mix the juice with the lemon sugar, the remaining sugar and the citric acid. Add the boiling water to make up to 3 litres, stirring until the sugar dissolves. Cool and store in the fridge.

To serve, dilute the cordial with cold water, mineral water or soda, and don't forget the lemon slices and mint leaves.

Christmas Eggnog

Serves 10–12

6 eggs
¾ cup sugar
1½ cups brandy
½ cup rum
600 ml milk
300 ml cream

Topping

300 ml cream
½ cup icing sugar
½ teaspoon vanilla
nutmeg, to garnish

Beat the cream, icing sugar and vanilla until thick. Just before serving, top each eggnog with a dollop of sweetened whipped cream and a sprinkling of nutmeg. Eggnog can also be frozen to make a great ice cream.

Separate the eggs and beat the yolks; gradually add the sugar and beat until pale and lemon coloured. Beat in the brandy and rum, then the milk and cream. Divide into cups or glasses.

Iced Orange Tea

Makes 6–8 glasses

6 Orange Pekoe or Orange Zinger tea bags
ice cubes
juice and grated rind of 2 juicy oranges or tangelos
mint leaves
ginger ale, lemonade, sparkling mineral water or soda water, to
    top up

Infuse the tea with 2 cups of boiling water, straining after 10 minutes. Place the strained tea, ice, orange juice and rind and mint leaves in a large glass jug and top up with the carbonated beverage of your choice. Serve in tall glasses with extra slices of mint to garnish.

Note: This recipe also works well with lemon-flavoured tea bags and fresh lemons.

Seabreeze Cocktail

A very refreshing, non-alcoholic, summer punch (without the punch).

1 part pineapple juice
2 parts Lemon and Paeroa
crushed ice
lemon and orange slices
mint leaves
1 can crushed pineapple (optional — difficult if using straws to drink)

Mix all the ingredients together in a jug and serve in tall glasses or champagne flutes.

Strawberry and Rock-melon Frappé

Take equal quantities of strawberries and seeded, skinned rock melon. Place in the blender, add ice cubes, and run the blender until the mixture is smooth and the racket stops. Garnish with fresh mint.

Homemade Ginger Beer

Makes 4 × 1.25 litre bottles

Brew your own ginger beer; it is not difficult and it tastes great.

Yeast Mixture

1 teaspoon dried yeast (not Surebake type)
1 tablespoon sugar
½ cup warm water

Ginger Beer

2 cups sugar
2 tablespoons ground ginger
1 teaspoon tartaric acid
2 litres hot water
juice and grated rind of 2 lemons
2 litres cold water

Stir the yeast mixture ingredients together in a small bowl or cup and leave to stand for 10 minutes. Place the sugar, ginger and tartaric acid in a clean bucket. Pour in the hot water and lemon juice, and stir to dissolve the sugar. Add the cold water, cool to lukewarm and add the yeast.

Leave in the bucket (covered with a towel) for 24–36 hours. Strain into 4 thoroughly clean 1.25 litre soft plastic drinks bottles. Fill the bottles to within 5 cm of the top with extra cold water. Put 1 teaspoon of sugar in each bottle, and screw on washed tops. Shake to dissolve the sugar.

Leave the bottles to stand in a warm place until they feel absolutely rigid when squeezed (this takes between 2–5 days to happen) then refrigerate. If the bottles are fizzy, loosen then tighten the lids several times. Consume within 2–3 weeks.

Irish Cream Liqueur

4 egg yolks
1 × 400 g can condensed milk
300 ml cream
3 tablespoons chocolate dessert topping (e.g. Cottee's thick and
  rich chocolate topping)
2 teaspoons coconut essence
450 ml whisky

Beat the yolks until they are thick and pale. Add all the other ingredients and beat until thick and well combined. Store in the fridge. Makes about a litre, enough for about 10 to 12 liqueur glasses.

Honey Peach Smoothies

Serves 2

1½ cups plain or peach-flavoured yoghurt
3 ripe peaches, peeled, pitted and sliced
2 tablespoons fresh lemon juice
1 tablespoon honey
splash of vanilla (½ teaspoon)
½ cup milk

Pour the yoghurt into an ice-cube tray and freeze until solid (about 4 hours). Purée the peaches, lemon juice, honey and vanilla, adding the milk to the mixture. Add the frozen yoghurt ice-cubes and process until the mixture is smooth and frothy. Pour into tall, chilled glasses and serve.

As a variation change the yoghurt favour and fruit type, for example, using strawberry, banana etc.

Index